Year *of* *the* Golden Dragon

B.L. SAUDER

COTEAU BOOKS FOR KIDS

Edited by Laura Peetoom
Cover and book design by Tania Craan

Library and Archives Canada Cataloguing in Publication

Sauder, B. L. (Bonita L.), 1961-   Year of the golden dragon / B.L. Sauder.

ISBN 978-1-55050-428-6

    I. Title.

PS8637.A7955Y43 2010   jC813'.6   C2010-901761-7

2517 Victoria Avenue
Regina, Saskatchewan
Canada   S4P 0T2
www.coteaubooks.com

10 9 8 7 6 5 4 3

Available in Canada from:
Publishers Group Canada
2440 Viking Way
Richmond, British Columbia
Canada   V6V 1N2

Available in the US from:
Orca Book Publishers
www.orcabook.com
1-800-210-5277

Coteau Books gratefully acknowledges the financial support of its publishing program by: the Saskatchewan Arts Board, the Canada Council for the Arts, the Government of Canada through the Canada Book Fund, the Government of Saskatchewan through the Creative Economy Entrepreneurial Fund, the Association for the Export of Canadian Books and the City of Regina Arts Commission.

For my family,
both East and West.

Hold fast your dreams!
Within your heart
Keep one still, secret spot
Where dreams may go,
And, sheltered so,
May thrive and grow
Where doubt and fear are not.
O keep a place apart,
Within your heart,
For little dreams to go!

Louise Driscoll
(1875-1957)

CONTENTS

The Curse
(China 210 BC – Days of Qin)

MASTER CHEN was teaching a lesson when he stopped in mid-sentence. His sleeping dog leapt up from its place at the hearth. It stood snarling at the door, ears erect, fur bristling along its spine. The dog slunk down and crept toward the thick, wooden door. Old Chen raised his hand and the animal halted, eyes fixed on the entrance.

Outside, the sound of distant drums rumbled. Chen and his two young apprentices froze as they listened to the low, echoing booms. The boys looked up at their teacher with eyes wide, waiting for him to speak.

Chen's lined forehead furrowed, and his jaw clenched. He narrowed his eyes but avoided looking at Xiao Long and Huang Li's faces as he pushed the children closer together. The teacher commanded the dog to stand in front of the two students.

Taking three long steps across the dirt floor, Chen grabbed his staff that was leaning against the clay wall. He gripped the pole with one hand and used the other to turn a black metal ring on the door, heaving it inward. The old man's eyes darted from side-to-side as he peered into the fog, which hovered close to the ground, covering everything with a veil of moisture. The damp earth and moss smelled rich – a perfect day to gather worms and centipedes for medicines. But there would be none of that now.

Chen stared in the direction of the Imperial Palace and sniffed. He turned to the dog. Its snout was raised into the air, acknowledging the smoke.

The drums had stopped.

Master Chen spun around, making his robe and its long, wide sleeves flutter. He snapped his fingers and pointed toward the door. The dog leapt to the entry and stood with its shoulders hunched forward, tail straight out.

Chen kneeled before the two boys, grabbing each one by an arm. He looked from one pale face to the other and said, "The drums in the capital city have been silenced. I fear the worst for your family."

The smallest child began to sob, but Chen did nothing to comfort him. He simply said, "We do not have much time."

Releasing the boys' arms, Chen reached for a small, square wooden box. The teacher said a few words and the lid sprung open. He took out a circular piece of jade hanging from a thin black cord. The flat jade disc was the color of a warm, green sea. Untying the cord, Chen removed the translucent stone and cupped it gently in his gnarled hands. The jade glowed, as if dozens of fireflies were captured inside.

"Come close," said Master Chen.

The children stared at the magnificent round pendant pulsating in their teacher's hands. A dragon and a phoenix, symbols of the emperor and empress, were engraved onto the pale green stone. The animals stared into one another's eyes, bodies curving downward, tails touching. Several tiny sections had been carved around the edges of the jade, like a delicate paper cutout.

Chen spoke in a deep voice. "Observe this royal emblem. It is beautiful, yes?"

The boys nodded, wide-eyed.

"The Emperor commissioned the best artist in the kingdom to create this pendant for your mother," Master Chen said, nodding toward the older boy. "The pendant was presented to her when you were one month old. It was created from a ball of jade that Black Dragon had given to the Emperor – a perfect sphere that the Emperor had promised never to carve."

The boys darted a look at one another.

"Please, Master. May I ask a question?" whispered Xiao Long.

"Yes," the old man said, glancing at the doorway.

"Mother was not the empress. Why did my father give her a pendant with a dragon and phoenix?"

"Your mother was the first wife to give the Emperor an heir," said Master Chen. "Not only did this gift enrage Black Dragon," Master Chen looked pointedly at Huang Li, "but also your mother, the Empress Ching."

Huang Li's eyes met Chen's for a moment before looking away.

"For many years now, the Empress has become obsessed with the idea that jade is known as dragon's stone because it enables dragons to live for hundreds, even thousands of years. Knowing that your father longs to be immortal, she believes that if she finds the correct jade, she will be able to offer him life everlasting. And in so doing, he will forget his other wives and love her best."

"Is that why the Empress broke the jade ball in the first place? She believed it had power inside of it?" asked Xiao Long.

"Yes," Master Chen said. "She thought the Emperor loved everything – you, your mother, even the jade from Black Dragon – more than her. So, during the days that the Emperor waited for his fourth wife to give birth to you, Xiao Long, the Empress grew more and more jealous and angry that the Emperor was spending so much time away from her. Infuriated, she took her ire out on the jade, cracking it open to see if it indeed held something inside. But there was nothing there.

"Your father was furious when he discovered what the Empress had done, and to pay her back for taking away the joy of your birth, he took the broken jade and had it made into a pendant so as not to waste its beauty."

Master Chen pursed his lips and looked into Xiao Long's face. "When your mother, Fourth Wife, died, the Emperor blamed it on the jade pendant. He brought it to me to lock away. Although the jade has been kept in a special box, it still has power to wreak havoc over your family. The time has come to try and suppress Black Dragon's anger which seeps from this jade."

Master Chen raised the pendant up in both hands, high above their heads. "Bow down and close your eyes," he commanded.

The children dropped to their knees and touched their foreheads to the ground. Their black braids trailed down their small backs as they huddled together, eyes squeezed tight. Master Chen's voice thundered above them:

> Dragon's treasure burning bright,
> In the darkness of this night.
> Once again it gives us light
> And speaks to us of its might.
>
> Dragon's treasure burning bright
> On this black and fateful night.
> Kings will never use its light
> Nor boast again of its might.
>
> Dragon's treasure burning bright
> Sear this image in their sight
> Royal sons must reach the height
> To rule with love, not with might.

There was a tremendous crack! The boys grabbed for one another.

"Stand up and open your eyes," Chen said to his pupils.

The half-brothers shook and gasped as Master Chen opened his hands. In his palms lay the pendant, no longer glowing, and broken into three pieces.

"Hurry," he said. "Each of you must take one."

With trembling fingers, Xiao Long automatically picked the section with the dragon. Huang Li took the piece showing the head of the phoenix. Master Chen put the last one into his pocket.

Chen bit the thin cord of leather that had been attached to the jade in half and hastily threaded a piece through pinprick holes in each piece of jade. He tied the pendants around each of the children's necks and tucked them under their heavy tunics.

"Let us go," he shouted, pointing towards the door, "Now!"

The boys ran out, the dog in the lead.

Master Chen reached into the fire and grabbed a burning log. He touched the fiery wood to his straw bed, low table and reed floor mats. They caught easily, smoking and curling as they burned.

The teacher moved quickly to a wall. Crouching down, he brushed a thin layer of dirt from the top of a stone slab. Pushing the stone aside he reached into a nook beneath and removed a paper scroll. The teacher was reaching for another scroll when he stopped. Out of the corner of his eye, he saw something move. A shape was forming in the black smoke swirling up from the fire. Chen shoved the scroll back underground and pulled the stone over the hiding place.

Master Chen stood just as black eyes formed in the smoke to glare at him from a horned beast's head. The creature spewed hot steam from its nostrils and yawned, revealing long, yellowed teeth inside a wet mouth. Its thick neck twisted and turned, extending into a snakelike body covered with shimmering scales. The dragon grew until it nearly filled the hut.

"Greetings, Master Chen." The sound was a low gurgle, as if from deep under water.

The animal circled the old man. Chen avoided looking into its flat, round eyes.

"Hail, Black Dragon, King of Dragons. To what do I owe the honor of this visit?"

The creature rolled its ebony eyes toward the palace. "The human leader, who calls himself Emperor, has wounded Black Dragon."

"Most dignified and esteemed guest," said Master Chen. "If I might ask my friend…"

"Friend?" Black Dragon roared, pressing his fanged jaws into the man's face. A smell like rotting fish eggs gushed from the beast's mouth as dollops of spit flew everywhere. The man remained still, trying to ignore what hit him in the face. "Master Chen has also hurt Black Dragon."

Chen cringed.

"Dragons and humans have long lived in divine balance. Black Dragon respected this ancient harmony. When this *emperor* gathered the humans under one ruler, Black Dragon was pleased since it is the correct way to keep men in their place. When this emperor asked Black Dragon to assist Chen in advising the throne, Black Dragon was pleased once more – as was Nu Wa, the creator goddess."

A low, deep groan erupted from the animal's long throat. As it shut its enormous eyes, a transparent film of skin and veins folded over them. The dragon bent its neck one way, then another. Back and forth, its monstrous head swung about the hut.

"Mighty Black Dragon only ever had one request," moaned the dragon. "My jade from Nu Wa was never to be altered or broken in any way. Still, when the Empress Ching broke my jade, Black Dragon found it in his heart to forgive the Emperor for his wife's evil deed.

"When you, my blood brother, kept the secret of the

Emperor making a necklace out of my precious jade, Black Dragon forgave Chen."

Master Chen glanced sideways at the growing flames.

The dragon sighed as it opened its reptilian eyes to thin slits. "The entire kingdom has knowledge of your 'second sight'. Could Chen not see the slaying of my dragon clan?"

"Venerable Dragon. Please, I am afraid I do not…"

"Silence!" Black Dragon roared. "Your emperor has ended the era of dragons and men living together in harmony. Tell this to your almighty ruler: 'An error of the present strikes the living; an error for the future strikes sons and grandsons.'

"I have destroyed the palace and its occupants. If anyone has survived, the rebels will finish them off." The animal snapped his jaws shut and snorted more steam through his wide nostrils. "To prove Black Dragon is not completely heartless, I will give humans a chance to rectify their forefathers' mistakes."

"Forefathers?" Master Chen asked softly.

Ignoring him, Black Dragon continued, "When the Year of the Golden Dragon meets the next millennium, Black Dragon will await the heirs of the Emperor and Master Chen. All of them, be it two or twenty, must come together to the river in the capital city to return the gift I once gave to the Emperor. It will be restored to its former shape as only Black Dragon has the power to do."

"Wise, Kind, Thoughtful, Generous Mighty Black Dragon," whispered Master Chen. "The Year of the Golden Dragon coincides with a millennium only once every three thousand years."

"Exactly," hissed Black Dragon. "Two thousand years from now."

"Surely Black Dragon —" Chen started to say.

The beast screeched, snorting hot, putrid vapors that filled the air. "If these humans fail to unite and return my jade, this day of hell will be repeated. Just as on this day, every man, woman and child will pay with their lives. Does Chen understand the magnitude of my loss now?"

Chen gagged and doubled over from the stench and impact of Black Dragon's words. Grasping his staff for support, Chen shook his head to regain his senses. He looked up at the flames licking the thatched roof.

Black Dragon was gone.

Master Chen stumbled to the door and saw the children astride their horses. The dog stood braced in front of them. The old master heaved himself up onto his horse, leaned forward and whispered into the animal's ear. The stallion reared up and lunged toward a break in the woods, leading the emperor's sons and Chen's faithful dog away from the roaring fire.

CHAPTER 1
The Lure

Hong Mei sat down at the computer and logged on to the Internet. She glanced across the café and saw the owner, Mrs. Wu, lighting a stick of incense. Hong Mei knew the grey-haired woman's routine. Every time Hong Mei entered the neighbourhood Internet café, Mrs. Wu started burning incense. It seemed that she, like everyone else, believed the gossip about Hong Mei, which was – Hong Mei stank!

Hong Mei's fingers pecked hard at the keyboard as she typed in a web address. Maybe I do smell, she thought, but who wouldn't? If they had to lean over bubbling pots of herbs everyday, they'd stink too.

The people in this town outside Beijing were as bad as every other place they'd lived in China. It didn't matter where she and Mama moved. Whether it was a bustling industrial centre or a serene fishing village, the locals always eyed the new arrivals with suspicion. From landlords to shopkeepers and neighbors, everyone was curious about the mother-daughter team and all were equally blunt.

"Where is your husband?" they'd ask her mother. "You are married, aren't you?" Or they might be a little subtler and say something like, "Hmm. You look awfully young to be a widow," hoping that Mama would give them some titillating gossip they could spread as soon as she and Hong Mei were out of sight.

But her mother never bothered answering their questions. She'd simply pull herself taller and stare down her perfectly straight nose at them. Her gaze would take in their inquisitive faces and travel slowly over their bodies. When she was done, Mama would nod with a slight smile on her lips. She would then speak very softly, in a bewitching sort of way.

She might say something like, "You shouldn't have to live with that painful knee," or "Have you been putting up with that sore back for long?" or whatever else her gold-flecked eyes and uncanny intuition told her. Of course, Hong Mei's mother was never wrong in her initial assessments and the unwelcome focus on her personal life would instantly shift to her inquisitors.

"Are you a doctor?" they'd ask.

"Yes," Mama would say. "I am a healer and I can cure anything." Of course, she wouldn't mention that her insight was supernatural or her vision better than x-ray. Even if people were curious as to how she read them so well, they were overcome with gratitude that someone was treating them for a bothersome ailment they'd often lived with for too long.

From toothaches or foot pain to insomnia or allergies, her mother had a remedy for everything. The longer she and Hong Mei stayed in a place — which usually wasn't very long — the better her mother's reputation as a healer would get. In a short while, people quit asking about Hong Mei's missing father.

Other than patients and their family members, Hong Mei's mother rarely talked to the townspeople. She made no friends. Most of their neighbours probably thought that Mama's desire for privacy was because of some past sorrow or tragedy that had befallen the mother and daughter team. In reality, it was fear.

Mama was always afraid that the secrets of their past would be discovered. In a land where marriage and family are the most important parts of *everyone's* life, people couldn't help but find it strange that a woman and her daughter were on their own. It was *unnatural* not to have a husband, grandparents or cousins around. Why was there no one else with them?

And if this worry was not enough, there was also the chance that someone would find out about Mama's magical powers of healing. Both she and Hong Mei knew that people were happy to be healed, but if they suspected it was through strange and mystical techniques, the authorities would no doubt be called in. And a single mother with a daughter to support didn't want to get thrown into prison, or worse, an insane asylum.

Under this shadow of dread, Hong Mei and her mother led their lives according to three strict rules: never keep written records of patients or the medicine Mama created; never share personal information with anyone; always leave town immediately if someone became too suspicious. And when they did flee, it was at night and always without saying goodbye.

Soon after they'd come to this village of Dong Hei, Hong Mei was helping her mother on her rounds. While her mother examined an old man at his home, Hong Mei heated a batch of medicine over a portable gas burner. It was always her job to make sure concoctions didn't stick to the bottom or boil over.

That day, while Hong Mei stirred the steaming brew, she heard, "What's that awful stench?"

Hong Mei stood up straight and saw a young girl standing in the front doorway. Hong Mei recognized her as one of the popular girls from school, probably the old man's granddaughter. She watched as the girl pinched her nose with one hand and waved the air in front of her with the other.

"I have never smelled anything so horrible," the girl said, wrinkling her nose in disgust at Hong Mei.

"*Dui-bu-qi,*" Hong Mei said, feeling her face burn. "I'm sorry. It's just the medicine."

Her schoolmate didn't bother listening. She just turned around and ran out of the house.

Hong Mei saw the girl at school the next day, chatting and giggling with some other students. As Hong Mei walked by them, they sniggered and squeezed their noses. Hong Mei turned away, hoping to hide her bright red face. She heard someone in the group say, "Phew! Even her hair stinks."

In the evening, Hong Mei hadn't bothered to ask her mother for a remedy for her *stench*. She knew her mother would only tell her the girls were being rude and to simply ignore them. So, without saying anything, Hong

Mei waited until all their neighbors were done using the apartment building's one bathroom. Armed with her mother's bandage-cutting scissors, Hong Mei stood before the broken mirror and chopped off her waist-long hair.

At first she thought her haircut looked quite good, but that was because it was wet. When it was dry, Hong Mei looked into the mirror and saw that it stood straight up. She tried to tame it by cutting it even shorter, but it was no use – the hair sprang right back up again.

Her mother was horrified when she saw what Hong Mei had done. "*Xiao Mei,*" Mama said, "*Wei-shen-ma?* Why did you do this?"

Hong Mei lowered her head and shrugged.

Her mother sighed. Hong Mei knew Mama could guess it had something to do with the girls at school. They'd both seen this kind of thing before. In one town, Hong Mei had been taunted for not having a father, another time for being the daughter of a *witch doctor.* In the last place, the children had teased Hong Mei about the tiny freckles that dusted her nose.

"Never mind," Hong Mei's mother said once she had got over the initial shock of Hong Mei's brush cut. "You are still my beautiful one." Mama then waved her hands slowly above Hong Mei's head and recited a chant:

> Long and jet black was the hair
> That crowned this head, now so bare.
> With these ancient words I ask,
> Make it grow, twice as fast.

"There," her mother said as she tucked her own stray wisps of ebony and silver hair back into a loose ponytail. "Repeat that as often as you can. It will make your hair grow."

Hong Mei said nothing.

"Maybe when you feel better," Mama said with a gentle smile.

The next day, after a good night's sleep, Hong Mei's mood was more optimistic. Before leaving for school, she said the chant and waved her hands over her head. She peered into the mirror, wondering how long it would take before she would see any growth. Well, she must at least smell better.

Later, when Hong Mei's schoolmates saw her, they said nothing about her smelling any different. In fact, they didn't talk at all, they were laughing so hard. When someone finally spat some words out, it was to call her a "needle animal." They laughed even harder after that.

Hong Mei walked away wishing she could have turned those girls into the hedgehogs they'd called her. Of course, she couldn't do anything quite that dramatic. Sure, she knew how to create huge red boils that would cover their bodies. Or perhaps she'd use the one that would give them an invisible rash to drive them crazy with its itch. Yes, she wanted to see them suffer…but using her mother's techniques in a devious way would be breaking her vow. Everything she learned from her mother had to be used for improving someone's life, not for making it worse.

Now, as Hong Mei sat in the near-empty café, she

reached up and felt the sharp, ink-black spikes of her hair. She pressed down on her head with both hands. Releasing them, her hair sprang back up again. Since she'd started using her mother's words every night, her hair was growing quite quickly – just not as fast as she wanted it to.

Hong Mei looked over at Mrs. Wu sitting at the coffee bar. She knew the woman wouldn't check up on her until the perfumed smoke drifted toward Hong Mei. Today, she was thankful for the old bat's insulting habit. It gave Hong Mei the time she needed.

After typing in her email address, she saw that, just like yesterday, she had mail. It was even from the same sender: Order of Monastic Studies – Beijing.

Opening it, Hong Mei read:

Dear Miss Chen Hong Mei,

As stated in our previous email, we wish to acknowledge that we have urgent information regarding your father. If you would like us to inform you of this news, we must first verify your identity.

The only true way of ensuring that you are the daughter of Chen Chu Lei is by having a small sample of your blood taken for DNA testing. Since you are sixteen years old and considered an adult under monastic law, you do not need a parent's permission to have the procedure done.

We must also reiterate how crucial it is to keep knowledge of this message and its contents to yourself. It is imperative that you do not share this information with ANYONE. If it is discovered that you have discussed any part of this communication, we will halt our process of reunification.

At this time of year, when all families come together to celebrate the Lunar New Year, it is our sincere wish that yours be one of these.

Please respond immediately to this email if you would like to be responsible for the happy and joyful return of your father.

Sincerely,
Madam Ching
Beijing Representative for the Order of Monastic Studies

Hong Mei unconsciously raised a finger to her mouth to nibble at the short nail of her pinky. Realizing what she was doing, she pulled her hand away, reaching instead into the front pocket of her jeans. She took out a small, milky-green piece of jade and placed it gently between her lips. The feeling of the cool stone made her forget about biting her nails.

Hong Mei had got the idea of using the jade to break her habit from a former teacher who had used the same technique to stop a student whispering the words she was reading. The teacher had told the girl to hold a pencil between her top and bottom lips.

Hong Mei found it worked equally well with either her flat, triangular stone or a writing instrument. But she was careful to only use a pencil or pen at home. She didn't want Mama finding out Hong Mei had her father's precious jade.

As she stared at the message before her, she thought back to the *gong fu* exercises her father had put her through when she was young. As she had grown older, Baba became more strict and demanding, often making her practice until she cried with exhaustion. That was when Mama tried to come to her daughter's rescue.

"Let her rest," Mama would say. "She is only a child."

"Yes, wife," he'd answer. "And she is only a *female* child."

Those words always made Hong Mei stop crying.

"She must work extra hard to overcome this disadvantage," Baba would say. "Chen Hong Mei represents a brave and noble clan. By being prepared, she will show respect to our ancestors when she meets Black Dragon."

At the mention of Black Dragon, Hong Mei would avoid looking at her mother, knowing what came next.

"I truly wish I had a remedy for madness," Mama would say to Hong Mei, "for I believe your baba is going crazy."

As always, this was the point the argument really got heated. "Crazy?" Baba would say, his brown eyes flashing dark. "You call me crazy for believing in Black Dragon? What about your spooky charms and strange spells? What makes them real and Black Dragon not?"

"Ssh! Keep your voice down, husband. You know that every time I cure someone, it proves the age-old magic behind my words."

This statement always seemed to make her father reconsider his words, or at least, to calm him down. But one fateful night, Baba's voiced swelled and filled their apartment, threatening to burst open the windows.

"Soon!" he boomed. "When the mighty Black Dragon walks among us, you will know the meaning behind *real* power."

That was one of the last arguments Hong Mei had witnessed and it had been several years and countless villages ago.

Hong Mei turned back to the email and hit the reply

button. She quickly wrote that she was Chen Hong Mei, daughter of Chen Chu Lei, and that she would be able to prove this by having her blood tested. She checked for mistakes and seeing none, she clicked *send.*

Hong Mei sat staring at the screen for a moment or two. Just as she was about to log off, Hong Mei noticed the yellow message light blinking in the corner of the screen. Hitting the button to retrieve the message, she saw that it was from the Order of Monastic Studies in Beijing.

That was weird. Was it an automated reply? Looking up, she searched for Mrs. Wu's steel-coloured hair. She saw the woman pointing at the clock on the wall. Hong Mei ignored her. Focusing on the computer screen again, she opened the email and started reading. It was a reply to her response. Her breath caught in her chest. How could they send her something so quickly?

Dear Miss Chen,

We have received your response and would like to inform you that you may have your blood tested in Beijing at 3:00 pm tomorrow afternoon.

Following are the directions to our institute, which is located within walking distance of Beijing Central Train Station.

Send us your response regarding this appointment as soon as possible.

Regards,
Madam Ching
Beijing Representative for the Order of Monastic Studies

Tomorrow? Right at the start of the Lunar New Year holidays? Shouldn't all colleges and institutes be closed by now? Her own school had already shut its doors.

Out of the corner of her eye, Hong Mei saw movement. Mrs. Wu was heading toward her. She definitely didn't want the old lady finding out about this. The news would reach her mother before Hong Mei even got home.

She looked back and forth between Mrs. Wu's pinched face and the computer screen. As the woman got closer, Hong Mei saw her lift a handkerchief to her nose.

Hong Mei typed in *yes* and scanned the directions to the institute before logging off. She jumped up, threw some money on the table and fled.

So what if the old biddy thought she stank. She'd show her.

CHAPTER 2

The Journey East

RYAN, WAKE UP! We're landing pretty soon," Alex said, elbowing his older brother in the ribs.

"Don't!" Ryan pulled the airline blanket up around his neck and edged closer to the window. The seat belt stopped him. Why did Uncle Peter always insist they keep their seat belts buckled for the entire flight? It made sleep practically impossible.

Ryan groaned and, with his eyes still closed, twisted his body back to face the front of the plane. His stomach growled. He wished he'd packed more snacks for the trip. He hadn't expected the airplane food to be quite so awful.

Shortly after taking off from Vancouver, they'd been served a dinner of stringy chicken, crusty rice and fruit salad. Thankfully, everyone had also been given one soft white bread roll. Ryan ate quickly, then told his brother to get him another one.

"Why me?" Alex asked. "You ask her."

"You're the one with the aisle seat. Hurry up or it'll be too late."

"Okay, okay. Don't panic," said Alex. "Excuse me?" he said, showing off a toothy grin. "Could my brother have another one, please?"

The stewardess looked back with an equally charming smile and said, "Of course. Would you like two more?"

"Okay. Thanks," Alex said as she placed the rolls onto their trays.

"Good job," Ryan said.

Alex eyed the untouched butter on Ryan's plate. "Can I have that?" he asked, pointing at it with his knife.

"Sure," Ryan shrugged. "You know I hate the stuff."

"Hate's a pretty strong word to use for butter," Alex said as he smeared the top of his roll with it. "Uncle Peter always says —"

Ryan cut him off. "Save the lecture. I've already heard it."

Sipping at some water, Ryan looked up at the television screen and put his headphones back on to continue watching the movie. The inflight magazine had labelled it as a comedy, but it was turning out to be a lot more like a *romantic* comedy. So far, he hadn't laughed once.

After awhile, he got bored and decided to sleep.

A short time later he woke up, his neck stiff and sore. He realized there was no question about it. He *hated* flying economy class and he didn't care if Uncle Peter thought that word was too strong. He knew those lucky passengers sitting near the front of the plane had fully reclining seats. He knew they had good food. And he knew they had better movies and video games. Someday he'd be old enough and rich enough to sit in Business Class — maybe even First Class.

Ryan reached forward to the seat pocket in front of him and felt for his wire-rimmed glasses. When he got to Nana and Yeye's, he was going to sleep for a week. That was after he'd eaten his fill of his grandmother's homemade *jiaozi*. He could taste the savoury meat-filled dumplings already. His stomach growled again.

He heard Alex giggle.

"What's so funny?"

Alex pointed at the sleeping couple across the aisle. Aunt Grace's head rested on Uncle Peter's shoulder, her blonde hair falling forward. Their uncle was sitting straight up with his head thrown back. The snores escaping from his nose and mouth were making everyone around them grin.

"Should I take a picture of them?" Alex asked.

Ryan nodded. His little brother looked so awake. How did he manage it? Had he slept at all?

Ryan watched Alex reach down to the bag stuffed under the seat in front of him. As he searched for his camera, his jade pendant swung out from under his shirt.

Alex stood up and leaned over Aunt Grace and Uncle Peter. He aimed his disposable camera at them and clicked.

The brightness of the flash woke his uncle, who snapped his mouth shut and blinked dark eyes at the two boys. Uncle Peter frowned and ran his fingers through his short black hair. He yawned and stretched, waking his wife.

"Put that thing away," mumbled Uncle Peter, but Alex only laughed and took another couple of pictures.

Uncle Peter lifted one eyebrow with feigned annoyance and unbuckled his seat belt before standing up.

"You guys better get cleaned up before we land. We're going straight out for dinner when we get there and I don't want to keep anyone waiting."

Ryan ignored the suggestion. There was no way he was going to use the bathrooms on this plane. They were usually okay at the start of the flight, but by now they'd be disgusting. He'd find a washroom after they'd landed. Everyone else could just wait.

He checked his watch. It was 7:05 PM Hong Kong time. He glanced at the overhead screen and read:

55 Minutes to Destination

Ryan could hardly wait to have a decent meal. They rarely got to eat *real* Chinese food. Alex and Aunt Grace's idea of "Oriental" food, as she called it, was sweet and sour chicken, egg rolls and chop suey. Uncle Peter had never learned to cook, so he and Ryan relied on trips downtown or to Richmond to seek out their favourite dishes. Who knew where his aunt and Alex went on those evenings if they didn't stay home – probably some Italian place.

Reaching over to the window, he pushed the blind up. He gazed out over the wing tip and saw the moon. It was almost full. Ryan tugged at the red silk cord around his neck and pulled out his own fan-shaped jade pendant, similar to the one Alex wore. He ran his finger along the scalloped edge first, then traced the two smooth sides. Glancing at the moon again, then back at the translucent, pale-green jade, he could understand how people in the old days thought jade was crystallized moonlight.

When asked, it was hard to explain to his friends why Chinese people were so crazy about jade. As for himself, if he told them he loved his pendant, they'd never let him live it down. But that's exactly how he felt. After wearing it for so many years, it had become a part of him. He dreaded the day he'd have to pass it down to the next generation.

Ryan thought back to his last trip to Hong Kong nine years ago, when he'd been nearly six years old and Alex was four. Mama, Papa, Alex and he were staying at his grandparents' apartment near a busy market. Papa had grown up in that neighborhood and he wanted to show his Chinese-Canadian wife and sons around.

Ryan remembered holding Mama's hand while Papa carried Alex. They walked through the market looking for things to buy for dinner that night. After getting some vegetables and fruit, the family wandered into the so-called wet market.

Even now, Ryan could still see the pails brimming over with slimy black eels, giant prawns and other wriggling sea creatures. There were pots filled with crab, abalone and giant sea cucumber. Crates overflowed with tiny dried shrimp, scallops and mussels. Farther on were wooden and bamboo cages stuffed with live chickens, ducks and geese.

When his father finished looking everything over, he pointed to a plump chicken and asked the butcher to prepare it for him. Ryan watched as the man grabbed the squawking bird, and with one hand, pinned it down on a bloody wooden slab. He grabbed an enormous cleaver and wiped it across his stained apron. Then, with one swift movement, he hacked clean through the fowl's neck. The beaked head plopped into a bamboo basket beside the chopping block, joining the rest of the feathered heads heaped inside.

Alex was too young to understand, but Ryan suddenly realized where a chicken dinner really came from. He remembered starting to howl and his father picking him up with his free arm. Papa had held him, together with little Alex, hugging and kissing them both. A few moments later, his father put both his sons down and ruffled their hair.

"You might look Chinese," Papa laughed, "but you sure can tell you're not from around here."

Now, as Ryan was about to visit Hong Kong again, a lump grew in his throat and his chest ached. He took his glasses off and pressed his forehead against the cold, black window and clasped his jade. He still missed his parents so much. It was seven years since they had died in the fire, but it seemed like only yesterday. He would do anything to see them one more time.

If someone could see into his heart, they would see that that was what he truly wished for.

CHAPTER 3

Anticipation

HONG MEI LEFT the Internet café and manoeuvred her bicycle into the lane reserved for cyclists. She noticed that traffic of both motor vehicles and bikes was heavier than usual. Everyone seemed to be out getting last-minute shopping or errands done before the holidays. Hong Mei didn't have to worry. She and Mama had already prepared for the New Year, or Spring Festival as many still called it.

First they'd cleaned their apartment, starting with the dust-covered ceiling fans and cobwebs in the corners of the room, and finished by scrubbing the wooden floors and beating the dirt from the worn carpets. Hong Mei didn't mind the annual cleaning binge since she, like most Chinese, thought that good fortune wouldn't find you if you hadn't "swept out the old to let in the new." She also knew that she had to clean everything before her mother would take her shopping.

This year she wanted to buy something really special to wear. After all, it wasn't just the Year of the Dragon coming up, but the Year of the *Golden* Dragon. She'd be 76 years old the next time there'd be another Golden Dragon year. Maybe she would be so old she wouldn't even be alive.

After a bit of a struggle, Hong Mei had finally convinced her mother they should both get different outfits rather than the typical red sweaters and skirts of previous years. Hong Mei wanted a pair of black jeans and a black turtleneck. Mama flatly refused, saying it was inappropriate for a young girl to wear all black. They compromised on black wool trousers and a red turtleneck with a tiny black dragon embroidered on it. Hong Mei was thrilled. It was by far the coolest outfit she'd ever owned.

When she and Mama finished buying clothes, they bought all their favourite New Year delicacies to prepare. There was a chicken to cook at home, long noodles and thin slices of juicy roasted duck. They bought both plain steamed bread and some filled with succulent barbequed pork and chopped onion and garlic. For dessert they chose an array of dumplings with sweet red-bean paste, crushed black sesame and puréed chestnut. Last, they filled tiny bags with watermelon seeds, dried plums and sugared walnuts.

Hong Mei helped her mother take the packages home. Then they both went out for the most important errand, the trip to the bank. The New Year wouldn't be complete without money being given and received.

Arriving at their small branch, Hong Mei and her mother saw that security guards were limiting the number of people entering the building. The next person in line was only allowed in when someone left the bank.

Mama shook her head and said, "Why do we always wait to the last minute to do this?"

Hong Mei shrugged. She didn't mind. Waiting to take out the crisp new bills was part of the lead-up to what she considered the *best* part of the New Year. And that was when *she* received her own money inside the small red *hong-bao*. Throughout the days of celebrating, neighbours and patients of her mother would stop by and give her small envelopes with bills of cash inside. Just the sight of one of the little packets could make her heart race. Although she was already a teenager, girls were given *hong-bao* until they got married, and she was a long way from that.

Plus, it didn't make any difference if she was stinky or not.

While they waited their turn at the bank to demand the newest and cleanest bills, Hong Mei watched her mother. She didn't have much money, but she would withdraw what she could. People didn't expect a single mother to give a lot of money, but custom demanded she give something.

Later, when they returned home and her mother prepared dinner, Hong Mei carefully smoothed and folded the banknotes to put inside the shiny red envelopes. She turned to her mother.

"How much lucky money for the trash collector, Mama? Should the doorman get more or less than him? What about the children next door?"

"Two bills for the trash collector, five for the security guard and one each for the children next door," her mother said. "Don't write their names on the envelopes until we have everyone's done."

"Yes Mama. I know," Hong Mei replied. She knew if she

missed someone, she'd risk not getting an envelope herself.

When they had finished, Hong Mei gathered up the pretty packages from the table. "Should I go now?"

"Yes. And don't forget to say *xie xie* when you receive your lucky money."

"I won't," Hong Mei had said as she skipped out the door that day.

Now, as Hong Mei pedalled home from the café, she thought about her mother. She worked so hard to support the two of them. Hong Mei knew that if she had been born a boy, everything would be different. Baba and Mama probably wouldn't have started arguing. Her father might not have become so obsessed with his belief in the return of Black Dragon. Maybe, Baba's monk brothers wouldn't have had to take him away.

Hong Mei felt butterflies in her stomach as she thought about going to Beijing the next day. There was absolutely no way she could tell her mother about any of it.

Now, what excuse would she use to get away? Hong Mei would have to find out what was missing from Mama's supplies and offer to get it before the holidays. What were they always short of? Soft-shelled beetles? Ridge-backed millipedes? Wait! Dragonfly wings. They were always running out of those.

And what a wonderful surprise it would be. She imagined walking into the apartment with Baba behind her. Would Mama burst out crying? Whom would she hug first, her or Baba?

Hong Mei turned the corner and rode into the apartment compound. She jumped off her bicycle and locked it up to the bicycle stand. When she reached their apartment door, she saw that her mother had decorated the entryway. Bright red bunches of firecrackers hung on either side of the front door. A shiny gold and red poster with the luck symbol was nailed to the door. To one side, a small fruit tree stood in a clay pot. There were twenty or thirty miniature oranges growing on the pretty shrub. Hong Mei bent to read the card tied to the orange tree. She smiled when she recognized the name. It was a gift from one of her mother's patients.

Hong Mei turned the doorknob and let herself in.

"Mama, I'm back!" Hong Mei called as she removed her shoes and put on a pair of slippers. She closed the door behind her.

There was no reply, meaning her mother was on a house call or perhaps giving out more *hong bao*.

Hong Mei moved past the green refrigerator which stood as a centrepiece in the one-room apartment. They'd never had a refrigerator before. This one was a gift from another of her mother's clients – a thankful father of twin boys that Hong Mei's mother had delivered. A vase of bright pink and red plastic flowers sat on top of the refrigerator along with several photographs of Hong Mei and her mother. There were no pictures of her father.

Hong Mei picked up an aluminum kettle and filled it with water from the kitchen tap. She turned on the gas burner and placed the kettle on the flame. While she waited for the water to boil, Hong Mei looked at the photographs.

There were several pictures taken over the years. The one Hong Mei liked best had been taken when she was a very little girl. Her hair was done up into two braids and tied with bright red ribbons. It was winter and she wore a quilted jacket. Her cheeks were rosy, either from the cold or a little rouge that Mama, like many Chinese mothers, had put on her child's cheeks. Small Hong Mei smiled into the camera as she clung to her mama's legs.

She suddenly thought of another time she stood clinging to her mother. That had been the last time Baba had been with them. The night Mama had secretly taken his jade pendant and thrown it away.

It had started when her father discovered his jade was missing. He couldn't remember where he'd taken it off, whether it was in their flat before he went to wash up or in the bathroom they shared with the other families.

When Baba asked Hong Mei's mother about it, she pretended not to know anything. Her father quickly became more and more anxious and searched everywhere for the pendant. Everywhere except the rubbish bin behind their apartment block.

Hong Mei was amazed that her mother didn't cave in and admit to what she'd done. She had *seen* Mama toss the jade into the rusty old garbage can. When Baba tried to use his second sight to trace his pendant and still couldn't find it, he started bellowing for anyone and everyone to hear.

"Where is it? Where is my jade? Someone has stolen my jade!"

Hong Mei's mother stood stoic and still.

Soon there was pounding at their apartment door. When her mother opened it, three men in dark monk's robes stood on the threshold. Hong Mei remembered that Mama seemed glad, maybe even a little relieved as she asked them inside. Hong Mei would never forget her father's reaction to the visitors. He immediately dropped to the floor and began kowtowing to them. The sight of Baba kneeling before these bald, stern-looking monks scared Hong Mei into motion.

Running to the back alley, she picked the pendant out from amongst rotting food scraps and other waste. She quickly rinsed the jade off at the outdoor tap and ran back inside.

Arriving back in their flat, Hong Mei saw that her mother hadn't moved to help or stand by her husband. But even odder was Hong Mei's sudden feeling that it was not her place to interfere either. Deep down, part of her wondered if she should say something about her father's jade, but something stopped her and she kept her mouth shut.

She gripped Baba's precious possession in one hand and clung to Mama with her other hand. Together, she and Mama watched the oldest looking of the men reach down and gently place his hand on her father's head. Baba looked up into the monk's face and nodded. Not a word was spoken.

A moment later her father stood up, smiled weakly at Mama and her, then turned and walked out the door, followed by the dark-robed men. When the last one closed the door after him, Hong Mei felt as if she'd just woken up from a dream. Realizing that her father was gone, she made a movement to go after him, but her mother held her firm. When Hong Mei looked up at her mother's face, she saw it was wet and glistening.

That night, she and Mama had also left home, never to return. To this day, they seldom talked about it. Hong Mei had asked her mother only once where the monks had taken Baba. Mama said she wasn't sure, but it would be a peaceful place for him to rest for as long as he needed.

Sometimes, Hong Mei would close her eyes and try to use her own second sight to see if she could see her father or where he was. It never worked.

For as long as she could remember, Hong Mei had seen things in her mind while the outside world seemed to disappear. They were similar to seizures in that she couldn't stop them. But they were also different, since people around her couldn't tell what was happening. Of course her father could, since she had inherited this trait from him.

When she was small, her visions usually lasted only a few seconds. They were images of celebrations such as birthdays or the Mid-Autumn Festival, and often contained glimpses of her parents or friends. However, it wasn't long before her visions began to change, becoming dark and scary. She was barely ten years old when she began seeing scenes of men dying in battle or women and children fleeing from intruders. And there was always fire. Fire and bodies.

Her visions seemed to come when she least wanted them, times when she was stressed or nervous. Her father insisted that they were a gift, and taught her techniques that his own father had shown him for taming his inherited second sight. She learned how to focus and breathe so that she could bring on images just by thinking about them. "By harnessing your visions," Baba said, "you make them your ally, not your enemy."

However, there were still plenty of times she could not manage them, and what she saw in her mind's eye became increasingly more frightening and unrealistic. At the same time, her father changed. From being loving and kind, he became more demanding during Hong Mei's *gong fu* training and preparation for what he called, "The Return of Black Dragon."

Now, Hong Mei reached into her pocket and took out the small, flat piece of jade and studied it. Not for the first time did she think it an odd shape for a pendant. Chinese favoured jade pendants that were circular, like flattened doughnuts or those old-fashioned Chinese coins with a hole in the middle. Some people wore a charm shaped like a peach, others a small Buddha or Goddess of Mercy.

Her father's jade was not like any of these. His had three edges, two straight as if they'd been sliced. The third side was carved with a wavy edge. It looked like a small Chinese fan.

What was even stranger than the shape of the pale green stone was what had been etched on its face: parts of two different animals – a bird and a serpent by the looks of it – but only the lower parts, claws, feathers and a scaly tail. It always made her wonder if this pendant was only one section of a more traditional circular piece of jewellery like her mother wore. But why would her father have kept a broken piece of jade? What had happened to the rest of it?

The whistle on the boiling kettle sounded. She sighed and put the jade back into her pocket. It seemed like she had been longing to see her father and ask him these questions for ages.

Hong Mei grinned to herself. It was lucky she'd kept them hidden in her heart for when she saw him again. As soon as they were reunited, she'd let them tumble out. He would understand immediately how much his daughter had thought about him.

CHAPTER 4

Sardine Class

ALEX DIDN'T HAVE TO FOLLOW Uncle Peter's advice about the toilet on the plane. He'd been using the one in business class for the whole trip. That stewardess was so nice. Not only had she let him use the washroom up front, but she must have given him ten cans of Coke during the flight. With all that sugar, he wondered if he'd be able to sleep when they went to his grandparents' after dinner.

Ugh! Dinner in Hong Kong: it was bound to be horrible.

Real Chinese food was something he tried to stay clear of. At a family reunion like tonight, there would be plenty of weird dishes. There was always at least one whole fish with head, tail and bulging eyes. For sure there'd be a roast duck complete with *its* head. And no doubt they'd have sautéed eel or squid or some other squirmy thing. Oh, and tofu. There was always tofu for Uncle Peter and Ryan. They loved that stuff.

Alex knew it was going to be bad, bad, bad.

At least Aunt Grace was normal. Alex couldn't imagine his aunt eating Chinese food more often than she absolutely had to. Tonight, she'd probably say she was tired and they'd get to go to Nana and Yeye's. But what if he got jet lag, like that time in Egypt? Uncle Peter had been pretty mad about that.

They'd been given all kinds of sweets and sodas on the flight to Cairo and had stayed awake the whole time. But once he and Ryan had got into the taxi, they'd crashed. Both of them had slept the whole way into the city and to their hotel. Alex had felt like a zombie as he stumbled through the corridors to their room. Through his sleep-induced fog, he heard Uncle Peter on the phone canceling the morning's camel trek.

After he hung up he said, "The whole point of flying business class is to sleep. Not to play video games for fourteen hours straight."

"Can't we just reschedule it?" asked Aunt Grace. "The Sphinx hasn't moved in over four thousand years. It'll still be there tomorrow."

"You know I have to be on-site for the rest of the week. If I miss the actual opening of the tomb, there's no point in my being here. Or on any other important dig, for that matter. Your inheritance won't last long if I lose my job."

That was the last thing Alex remembered before waking up later that afternoon.

Uncle Peter got over it, but he was still angry enough that he vowed that Aunt Grace wasn't going to "waste any more money buying Ryan and Alex business class seats." They would go back to flying what he and Ryan called "sardine class."

There was no use in begging Uncle Peter to change his mind. He'd only say, "When you're a parent you can make decisions about your own family. Until you and Ryan are old enough to leave my house, you'll live by my rules."

Alex laughed a little now and loosened his seat belt. Uncle Peter was always saying things like that, but he was actually a real softy. He'd taken Ryan and him in, hadn't he? Everyone told his brother and him how lucky they were to have such great "parents." It was true, he guessed. He liked living with Uncle Peter and Aunt Grace.

Their house was in West Vancouver, at the foot of the mountains on the North Shore. When he wasn't at school, Alex was at nearby Westwood Riding Academy working with Rubicon. Technically speaking, the ebony mare belonged to Aunt Grace. But after buying Ruby with the first of her inheritance, Aunt Grace had only taken a few lessons before she – as she said – "got busy with the boys." That was just after he and Ryan had come to live with them.

He remembered Aunt Grace letting him sit on Rubicon as the instructor led the horse around the arena. Alex cried when he got off after a few laps. He must have known already that he and Ruby were meant for each other. Ever since then, Rubicon did exactly what he asked her to. Whether it was by using the reins or whispering in her ear, Alex and his mare were on the same wavelength. Someday, he hoped to race with her, but he'd have to wait until he was older for that.

Yeah. Life was good with Uncle Peter and Aunt Grace.

If he was to tell the truth, he never really thought about Mama and Papa. Unlike Ryan, he didn't remember that much about them, or about the fire.

He glanced over at Ryan looking out of the plane window. As usual, he was in his own world. Alex felt a stab of shame. He wondered why he didn't miss their parents as much as Ryan did.

"Hey, Alex," he heard Aunt Grace say softly from across the aisle.

He grinned over at her. "How'd you sleep?"

"Horribly," she yawned. "And you?"

"I didn't."

"Alex!" Aunt Grace said, watching her husband walking back toward them from the toilet. "Your uncle is going to kill you if you fall asleep during the reunion dinner."

Uncle Peter reached his seat, sat down and immediately did the seat belt back up. He looked at them and then narrowed his eyes. "What? Did I miss something?"

"No. Nothing," Alex and Aunt Grace said simultaneously.

Alex liked being on Aunt Grace's side. Even when he was really young, he'd felt like they had something special. He thought back to when their adoption went through. That was also the day Uncle Peter had given Ryan and him their jade.

His uncle still wore glasses back then, and when he had held out the two pendants toward the boys and began to explain the legend behind them, his uncle's eyes had looked sad, Alex thought.

Alex remembered, too, how he had snuggled up to Aunt Grace and asked what a legend was.

"It's a very old folk tale," she whispered.

The Wong family legend was that the jade pendants were two parts of a whole. With a third part, the jade formed one complete disc – but that piece had been lost long ago.

What had stuck in Alex's young mind most from the tale was that the original, whole piece of jade once belonged to one of China's first emperors. Nobody knew how the jade had ended up in their family. Uncle Peter said the boys' father had a theory, but all the proof had been destroyed in the fire.

Alex would never forget how Ryan had glared at him then. Alex had immediately started crying while Uncle Peter explained, not for the first time, that the fire was an accident and that Alex had nothing to do with it.

Over the years, Uncle Peter added information to the legend – for example, that their father had gone back to their grandfather's village in China where he was given an old scroll. The poem written on it was in a very old style, but he'd had it translated into both modern Chinese and English, especially for his sons. He had often recited the English version to them. Ryan loved it and had memorized the entire poem. At the time that Papa and Mama died, Alex knew only a few lines:

> A man stood ashore, watching the sight
> Of mighty Black Dragon in the moonlight.
> The man was drawn by the pale green stone,
> And vowed at once to make it his own.

After the fire, Ryan refused to recite any part of the poem, and wouldn't even stay in the room if Uncle Peter mentioned it. Alex ended up learning it by himself from a copy Uncle Peter had.

Looking over at Ryan as he stared out the window, Alex hoped this trip would make his brother feel a bit better about losing their parents. Alex thought that if he could have just one wish, he would ask for that – something to make Ryan forgive him for something he'd never even done.

CHAPTER 5

The Poisoned Apple

HONG MEI STOOD on a sidewalk in Beijing, the capital city, where emperors and empresses once ruled. Instead of the rickshaws and sedan chairs of days gone by, there were cars, taxicabs and crammed buses clogging the busy road behind her.

There were also throngs of people riding bicycles, many of whom wore white surgical masks to protect their noses and lungs. It had been a dry winter with little snow, so the sands blowing down from the Gobi Desert had arrived early. The already polluted air was thicker than usual.

Hong Mei shivered and pulled her collar up. She'd be happy when spring arrived.

Squinting at the number plate on the drab building in front of her, she wondered why the Order of Monastic Studies, especially with its auspicious address, 188, didn't have a more impressive entrance. The single door she stood before was in the centre of a narrow, windowless structure, wedged between two high-rises.

188. She was sure that had been the address in the email. They must not want too many people to notice it was there.

Hong Mei was about to start biting one of her ragged fingernails, but she caught herself. Instead, she reached into her pocket and felt the familiar grooves of her jade talisman. Just the feel of it made her feel better.

She climbed the few steps and looked for a doorbell or buzzer. Not seeing one, she was about to knock on the door when it swung open.

A man with a shiny skull and deeply wrinkled face peered out at her. "Yes? What do you want?"

"Is this the Order of Monastic Studies?"

Instead of answering her question he asked, "Who are you?"

"My name is Chen Hong Mei. I have an appointment —"

"Yes, yes. Come in."

The stooped man waited for her to enter before shutting the daylight out. Hong Mei caught a glimpse of a corridor leading away from the tiny foyer where she stood. She saw a few closed doors along either side of the hallway, but heard no voices.

The sound of the man locking the door startled her and she turned around. He was already right behind Hong Mei, but he moved closer, peering intently at her.

Hong Mei backed away.

"Hmm," he said. "Why is your hair so short?"

Before she could say anything, he pointed at her face. "What are those brown dots on your nose?"

Hong Mei felt herself blush. "Excuse me, sir, but they're freckles. Many people have them."

The man looked unconvinced. "Too much sun, if you ask me."

Hong Mei wanted to say, "Who asked you?" but held her tongue.

"Follow me then," the man said as he shuffled down the long, dark hallway.

The only sound Hong Mei heard were their footsteps on the wooden floorboards, muffled in the tunnel-like space. The air seemed just as dusty as outside and Hong Mei stifled a sneeze. Looking up, she noticed a sliver of light from a narrow skylight high above.

When they came to a door with a folding chair beside it, the man said, "Have a seat. I will tell them you are here."

He opened the door and shut it softly behind him. Hong Mei sat on the edge of the hard metal seat.

Hong Mei squirmed on the uncomfortable chair as the minutes ticked by. She wondered how long this was going to take. Looking at her wrist, she remembered her watch was broken. Maybe she would use some of her *hong bao* money to get it fixed.

Hong Mei peered up at the slim band of sky through the skylight. It was already getting dark. She'd never been in Beijing alone at night.

The door beside her creaked open and Hong Mei leapt up. She remembered her manners, however, and waited for the old man to invite her in. He motioned for her to enter. Hong Mei felt his eyes studying her face as she walked past him.

The room was windowless and even darker than the corridor behind her. She could barely make out the outline of a long table. Hong Mei smelled something. Sandalwood?

She heard a *click*. A desk lamp was switched on, creating a tiny patch of light on the table. She could see the silhouette of a person sitting behind it, but not a face. Hong Mei focused and saw the outlines of two more people sitting on either side of the central figure. They also turned on lamps, illuminating pale circles on the hard surface of the table.

"May we have a light for Miss Chen, please?" she heard a deep, female voice ask from behind the middle light.

There was a very loud *click* before Hong Mei was suddenly blinded. She lifted both hands to her eyes, trying to shield them from the bright white light above.

"*Dui-bu-qi,* sorry," said the same husky voice from the other side of the table. "We just want to get a good look at you."

As Hong Mei stood in the spotlight, she thought about how she must look. Perhaps she should've worn a skirt instead of her New Year's outfit. Would her father think it was strange her hair was so short? She hoped he remembered her freckles and wasn't as disgusted by them as the old man obviously was.

"That's enough. Please turn down the light."

The room immediately dimmed and Hong Mei blinked to clear her vision. When she looked toward the table again, she saw the old, bald man sitting amongst the others. A woman in the centre stood up. Her face and upper torso were illuminated from below, giving her face unkind shadows. Still, it was obvious that the woman was beautiful.

She was tall and held herself so straight that she reminded Hong Mei of a statue. Her jet black hair had been pulled up high, coiled into an elaborate pretzel shape on the top of her head. She wore a shimmering teal robe, and when she moved even slightly, the material flashed green, then blue and gold. At her waist and around the wide cuffs of her billowing sleeves the cloth was scarlet, shiny and rich like a ruby. *Like an empress.*

As if to answer Hong Mei's thoughts, the woman introduced herself. "I am Madam Ching." Then she motioned vaguely to her left and right and said, "These are members of the Order."

Members of the Order?

The woman smiled and continued in her smoky voice. "I suppose you are wondering why there are women amongst us. Surely your father told you of female warriors."

Hong Mei nodded, trying not to frown.

"You see, Miss Chen, it was decided that not only would we would check your blood for verification of your lineage, but we would also interview you as well. You don't mind answering a few questions, do you?"

The way Madam Ching said this made Hong Mei's legs go rubbery. She forced herself not to raise a hand to her mouth. Instead, she reached into her pocket and clasped her jade. Its coolness steadied her.

"I am sure you are well aware that we will soon be entering the Year of the Dragon; the Year of the *Golden* Dragon, to be precise."

Hong Mei could hear the other people shifting in their seats.

"Can you tell us what is so significant about this Dragon Year?" Madam Ching asked in a silky tone.

Hong Mei's stomach lurched. Her forehead was suddenly damp, and she could feel the moisture forming under her arms. She wanted to take a deep breath, but it seemed like there wasn't enough oxygen in the room. She tried to remain calm by staying focused and drawing in tiny puffs of air through her nose.

When Hong Mei managed to find her voice, it came out as a whisper. "Well, the regular Year of the Dragon rotates every twelve years. But Golden Dragon years only come along once in a sixty-year cycle."

"Yes, yes. Every Chinese knows that," the elegant woman snapped. "Is there anything else?"

"I don't think so," Hong Mei said, trying to avoid the woman's gaze.

"Tsk!" Madam Ching clicked her tongue sharply and sat down.

Hong Mei began to hear a buzzing in her ears. Her scalp felt hot under the light, and her back began to itch as a trail of sweat trickled down her spine.

Next to Madam Ching, a tiny woman grasped the edge of the table, pulling herself to a standing position. She seemed no taller than when she was seated. The knot at the top of her head held the last few strands of her snow-white hair and her earlobes seemed stretched, weighed down by the deep-yellow gold earrings she wore. She smiled a little.

"My dear child," she croaked. "We only wish to see your family reunited once again. Although your father's removal from your home was a last resort, please under-stand that it was necessary in the lead-up to the Year of the Golden Dragon. We are very nearly there and he is about to go home with you. You must, however, answer our questions honestly and sincerely. Now, please tell us about your martial arts training."

"My father taught me when I was little," Hong Mei mumbled. She felt as if she were burning up. The overhead light and strong smell of sandalwood were making her feel faint. She knew her face must be crimson.

"Your father told us that you have studied advanced fighting. That's quite different than what a *normal* young person learns, particularly a young girl. Isn't it?"

Hong Mei was silent, trying to steady her mind with the tiny puffs she was working in and out of her nose. Perhaps she shouldn't have stopped practising all that *qi-gong* and other breathing exercises she used to do. Shrugging, the woman sat down and Madam Ching stood up again.

"Miss Chen," she began evenly, "this is extremely important. I must break all protocol and not waste any more time with niceties. According to our information, we are quite confident that we know who you and your father are. Do you?"

Hong Mei swallowed. What did the woman mean?

Madam Ching snorted and said, "Let me get to the point. You must be familiar with the tale of Black Dragon."

Black Dragon?

The woman reached into one of her wide sleeves and removed a scroll. As she unrolled it, Hong Mei could see that the yellowish paper looked very old and fragile. Some sections appeared to have been torn away, especially around the charred edges.

Madam Ching stopped to put on a pair of glasses, resting them near the end of her nose. Gazing over the tops of the lenses at Hong Mei, she began to recite:

> Long before the universe was born,
> Chaos rose from a celestial storm.
> Alone for eons in an endless night,
> The god awoke and created light.

Hong Mei thought of her father and closed her eyes. As soon as she did, she felt the familiar prickling along her hairline and tickle at the nape of her neck. Her mind's eye was about to start working again. A vision was coming.

Standing now amongst strangers, the room and its occupants seemed to fade away. Hong Mei no longer heard Madam Ching's voice.

Behind Hong Mei's closed eyelids, she began to see the colour red. Not the lustrous New Year's red that went with pretty gold writing. Neither was it like the lanterns that hung in the doorways of restaurants, nor the embroidered red of a bride's silk wedding gown. No, this was black-red. Dark and thick, it flowed like a sluggish river.

As Hong Mei's vision continued, she knew instinctively that what she saw was blood. The red current spread over cobbled streets and dirt roads. Then she saw people, dead or dying, moaning and crying for help.

Hong Mei felt as if she were going to collapse.

She began to hear Madam Ching's voice again as the woman recited other lines of the poem that Hong Mei knew so well:

> Hail, Black Dragon. I'm Emperor of this land.
> What? Dragon hissed, tail swishing in the sand.
> Chaos made *me* ruler of land and beasts.
> I did not see *you* at that happy feast.

49

True, said the Emperor, 'twas before my time.
The world has since changed, land and men are
now mine.
'Tis the first I've heard of this, Black Dragon said.
Deep within his heart he felt the fist of dread.

The horrible scenes that had rushed into Hong Mei's
head began to ebb, but they left in her mouth a taste of old
metal and rust. She wanted to spit.

"Miss Chen?" asked Madam Ching. "Shall I continue?"

A chill raised goosebumps on Hong Mei's arms. She
hugged herself for warmth and shook her head.

Madam Ching leaned forward slightly and dropped
her voice as if she were sharing a secret. "You know about
Black Dragon's jade, do you not?"

Baba's story couldn't be true, could it?

"We know who you are," Madam Ching said. "It is
going to be all right, for we are here to help you. You
realize, of course, that you are one of the heirs chosen to
return Black Dragon's jade?"

"I don't know what you're talking about."

"I think you do."

Hong Mei was scared. "I want to see my father."

"Oh, you will," Madam Ching purred, looking nonchalantly at her extremely long, red nails, "as soon as you
fulfill your obligation." She smiled. "The scroll is proof
that Black Dragon existed – and most likely still does, since
dragons live for hundreds of years. He is probably close
to the age when a dragon must, how shall we say, *expire*.
According to the pact between Master Chen and Black
Dragon, we know what the monks and your father have

always known – you are the one chosen to give back the jade to Black Dragon before he dies."

Hong Mei shook her head in disbelief. "I don't know anything about any jade. My father only told me I would be *meeting* Black Dragon some day."

Madam Ching narrowed her eyes. "Don't be coy. You must know where *part* of Black Dragon's jade is. Your father wore it for years!"

Hong Mei fought the urge to put her hand into her pocket and hold the stone. *Baba's jade belonged to Black Dragon?*

Sighing heavily and scowling, Madam Ching said, "Perhaps we should contact the authorities and get them to question your mother –"

"No," Hong Mei said, feeling her temperature rising. "She doesn't know where the jade is, but –"

Madam Ching smiled very slowly. "But you do, don't you, Miss Chen?"

Hong Mei felt as if someone had punched her in the stomach. Her shoulders sagged and she let her head drop.

"Now, now. There's no need to feel bad," Madam Ching said as she clapped her hands twice. "You should be excited, young lady. This is an honour!"

The rest of the people at the table slowly rose and filed out of the room. When only she and Hong Mei remained, Madam Ching said, "We have discovered that the other two pieces of Black Dragon's jade are with the Emperor's heirs."

"Other pieces? *Emperor's* heirs?"

Madam Ching ignored her and continued. "The heirs are on their way to Hong Kong as we speak. All *you* must do is meet them and escort them here to the capital – with their jade, of course. You will fly to Hong Kong immediately."

Hong Kong? Hong Mei's mind reeled.

"To ensure that everything goes as planned, you will travel alone and not discuss this with anyone. I will remain here in Beijing, close to your mother and father."

Madam Ching tilted her head. The action made Hong Mei look at the woman's old-fashioned hairstyle more closely than she had before. It looked like one of those wigs women wore in movies about ancient China. Why was she dressed like that? Weren't people from monasteries supposed to not care about clothes and fancy hairstyles?

"Of course your father is very excited about seeing you again," Madam Ching went on, "but I cannot allow you to speak with him just yet. It is only my vows to the monastery that causes me to be so strict in this matter."

Hong Mei's eyes filled with tears and her mouth twitched.

"If you are a true Chen, you will work with your family's legendary skills to entice the heirs to come to Beijing. Then, when this is accomplished, the three of you will use your jade as bait – I mean – as a way of convincing Black Dragon to come to the capital. He will be thinking he is coming to retrieve his jade, but we will also have a chance to prove to the world that Chinese dragons really do exist."

"Why can't I go and get the other two pieces of jade and bring them back by myself?"

"Because, Miss Chen, that is not the way I wish it to be done. Nor is that the way it has been written. Perhaps your father didn't have a chance to go through this with you?"

"When do you need to do my blood test?"

"There's no need. We already know who you are."

"What if I say no?"

"That's entirely up to you, Miss Chen, and whether or not you wish to see your father again." Madam Ching turned and glided toward the door. "It is your destiny, dear. It always has been."

Hong Mei felt tears flood her eyes. Her whole world was toppling over. How could she have been so stupid?

Madam Ching stopped to look back at Hong Mei. "I'm sorry. It was not my intention to be cruel. You may write a note to your mother saying you have left home 'to sort some things out' or something like that. Tell her that it is a surprise and you will return home after the New Year. Your parents are going to be so proud of you!" Madam Ching turned gracefully on her heel. "I'll leave you alone for a few moments to write your letter. When I return, I will give you more explicit instructions."

As soon as she left the room, Hong Mei heard the bolt slam on the other side.

She collapsed onto the floor and pulled her body into a tight ball. Why had she responded to that email? Did she really have to do this alone? Why couldn't her father help her? And did he, wherever he was, still have his second sight?

If he could use it, would he see her here on the ground?

She pulled herself together and stood up, brushing off her clothes. Madam Ching was right. This was her destiny, and Hong Mei knew it.

CHAPTER 6

East Meets West

MOMENTS AFTER the jet touched down in Hong Kong, Alex stood up.

"Sit down!" Ryan said, pulling at the hem of Alex's jacket.

"Why? Nobody else is."

Alex was right. Everyone was either getting up or already pushing into the aisles to get their bags and duty-free goods from the overhead bins. After such a long flight, passengers just wanted to get off the plane.

Ryan remained seated and looked down at his wrinkled clothes. Before leaving for the airport, he'd put on a crisp white shirt and carefully tucked it into pressed khaki trousers. He wondered why he'd spent so long ironing his clothes. They were a mess now.

After they got their luggage he'd find a washroom and change into the clean shirt he'd packed in his carry-on bag. He hoped that the bathroom at the airport was okay since he also wanted to brush his teeth. That was the one thing that bothered him about travelling. Public washrooms in some countries were pretty bad. Sometimes they had running water but lots of times they didn't. And they *never* had toilet paper. If Aunt Grace was with them, it was okay since she was always prepared. Her handbag had everything from menthol-scented tissue to instant hand sanitizer to super-fast-acting antihistamines – just in case someone developed a nasty allergy or got bitten by some weird bug.

Ryan reached into his pocket and pulled out a small tin of mints. These were his key to travelling survival. If he couldn't shower and brush his teeth, he had the backup of breath-freshening candies. He liked these super-strong ones best. Ryan popped one of the powdered peppermints into his mouth. It immediately released its powerful flavour. He had to hand it to the Brits. They totally understood peppermints. They made the best ones around.

He glanced at Alex with his Roots sweatshirt and backward-facing baseball cap. The logo on his cap read: "I am Canadian."

No kidding. As if everyone won't be able to tell.

Finally, the doors of the plane opened. Ryan and the rest of his family pushed their way off the plane along with everyone else. Chek Lap Kok airport in Hong Kong was still fairly new and could easily accommodate thousands of travellers. Still, every square metre of the building seemed filled with people. Chinese and foreigners from around the world had descended on the city to celebrate the Lunar New Year.

Newly arrived tourists moved toward a long bank of customs officers. Children and adults alike gawked in delight at the fabulous array of decorations. Giant, bright-red bunches of firecrackers and glowing, bulbous lanterns dangled from the towering ceiling overhead. Intricately carved gold, yellow, red and blue paper animals appeared to float on the air above the newcomers: giant tigers, monkeys, snakes, and other animals of the Chinese zodiac greeted guests.

And more beautiful than any of the others were the enormous, shiny gold dragons, eyes burning electric red, reminding everyone that this – the Year of the Golden Dragon – was what everyone was there to celebrate.

Clang!

"Hey, guys! Do you hear what I hear?" Uncle Peter asked, looking around.

Clang! Clang! Bong!

The sounds of the gongs and cymbals were getting louder.

"There it is! It's coming this way!" Alex shouted as the bright, rainbow-coloured lion shook and shimmied its way through the crowd. Ryan spied the men's real legs under-neath, dressed in black trousers and slippers.

Clang! Clang! Bong!

The round, dog-like face bobbed up and down, bat-ting its long-lashed eyes at the audience. First, the lion would stretch high into the air, then, shaking its white, furry head, it would crouch down low. The rest of its body swayed and slithered to the sounds of twanging musical instruments and brass gongs.

Ryan couldn't help smiling as he watched the perfor-mance. It had been a long time since they'd seen a Lion Dance. When the lion got to the Wong family, it stopped directly in front of them. The person inside the front of the lion's costume bent down low, like he was bowing.

Ryan let himself laugh. "I guess it likes us."

Everyone around them grinned.

Uncle Peter looked toward the customs counter. "C'mon," he said. "It's our turn."

Ryan looked back at the lion as they moved up to the glass booth. Uncle Peter slid the four passports through a narrow metal slot toward the female officer inside.

Ryan felt Alex nudge him and say under his breath, "Check *her* out!" He motioned toward the immigration officer.

Looking at the young woman with long, licorice-black hair, Ryan said quietly, "She's out of your league. And I'd say she's a bit old for you."

Her eyes were cast down at the documents before her. When she looked up through heavy, black-framed glasses, her eyes met Ryan's. Her pretty face immediately turned scarlet before she quickly looked down again. She let her hair fall forward, shielding her face from him.

She *was* pretty! For once, he and Alex agreed on something. Ryan could still see part of her nose with its delicate dusting of tiny brown freckles. She looked a little like that TV star. Ryan watched the young woman push the unopened passports back toward Uncle Peter and noticed her badly bitten fingernails. He heard Alex whisper up at Uncle Peter. "Isn't she, like, going to stamp them?"

Uncle Peter said, "I think you forgot to stamp our passports, Miss."

The officer looked confused.

Uncle Peter tapped on the glass and pointed at the big, round chop and inkpad sitting on the desk in front of her.

"Ah! Right!" the young woman said as she grabbed hold of the stamp. She opened their passports and hastily stamped each one, barely looking at what she was doing.

Thump. Thump. Thump. Thump.

She pushed them back toward the family, mumbling, "*Gong-Xi-Fa-Cai!*"

Gong-Xi-Fa-Cai?

Ryan saw confusion on Uncle Peter's face, too, as he mumbled "*Gong-Xi-Fa-Cai*" in response.

"Cool." Alex said beaming. "People really do speak Chinese here."

"Yeah," said Ryan, looking up at Uncle Peter, "but I thought you said they spoke Cantonese here. Wasn't she speaking Mandarin?"

"Yes. You're absolutely right," said Uncle Peter smiling widely. "I guess some of those Mandarin Chinese lessons have paid off. I told you more people would be using Mandarin in Hong Kong now."

Ryan was disappointed. He'd wanted to use what little Cantonese he remembered speaking with his parents.

He turned around to look back at the immigration officer and saw that she was standing up and leaving the booth. Where was she going? He wished his Chinese, either Cantonese or Mandarin, was better.

Ryan quickly caught up to the rest of his family and heard his Aunt Grace complaining.

"Look at this!" she said. "That girl stamped the wrong page. I knew she didn't know what she was doing."

Ryan saw Uncle Peter frown at his wife.

"Well, it's true!" Aunt Grace said. "No wonder, either. She hardly looked old enough to babysit, let alone have that uniform on!"

Ryan tried to ignore the exaggerated wink Alex made at him.

"What'd I tell you?" Alex asked.

"Oh, be quiet," Ryan said, moving away from Alex to get closer to Aunt Grace. Ryan put his arm lightly around her shoulders and looked Aunt Grace in the eyes – something he'd finally grown tall enough to do. "Well, Auntie. You always say Chinese people look younger than they really are."

"Ryan!" Grace said, trying not to smile. "I do not!"

He smiled and said, "Just kidding. I know you don't think we all look the same either."

"Peter!" Aunt Grace exclaimed, "Have you heard the words coming out of your nephew's mouth?" She started laughing and tugged Ryan's hand still resting on her shoulder. "You are terrible."

"Okay, everybody," Uncle Peter said. "Now's not the time to debate the difference between East and West. Stay together and nobody will get lost. Let's go and get our luggage. Hong Kong awaits us!"

Ryan walked out of the washroom near baggage carousel number twenty-seven. A sign was posted above the rotating luggage with "Flight CX183-Vancouver" printed in lighted letters. He wore a clean shirt, his hair was combed and his face washed. He ran his tongue over his freshly brushed teeth. He felt good. Well, maybe not good, but better.

Where was Alex? He was supposed to be watching for their suitcases.

There he was – standing in front of a screen showing flight arrivals. Ryan walked over. As he neared his brother, Ryan heard him reading out loud, "British Airways, China Airlines, Lufthansa, Cathay Pacific, Singapore Airlines, Cathay Pacific. That's five Cathay, three China Airlines, and two Singapore. Or is that three from Singapore?"

"What are you doing?" Ryan asked.

Alex didn't bother answering. Instead, he reached up, took his cap off, scratched his head and pushed his thick, black bangs back.

"I thought you were supposed to be watching for our luggage," Ryan said. "I also thought you were supposed to get your hair cut before we left Vancouver."

"One: I didn't see any barbers. Two: I ran out of time."

"Too busy playing with your pony friends?" Ryan asked.

"At least I *have* friends," Alex said.

"One day you'll find out there's more to life than horses."

Alex rolled his eyes and looked back at the screen. "Yeah, whatever," he said. "Anyway, I thought I'd just get my hair cut while we're here."

"What? You can't get your hair cut during Chinese New Year," Ryan said. "You'll have bad luck for the entire year!"

Alex snorted, "Yeah, right!"

"Nobody's going to cut it, you know," Ryan said,

trying to hide some of the annoyance in his voice. He hated when Alex got under his skin.

"Aunt Grace'll find someone to do it for me," Alex said.

"Aunt Grace will find someone to what?"

Ryan turned to see his aunt had joined them. She had pulled her hair back into a ponytail and put lipstick on.

"Get my hair chopped," Alex smirked.

"Of course, darling," Aunt Grace said. "We don't believe any of those old wives' tales, do we? I'll find a place we can both go to – a haircut for you and a manicure for me. Now, Ryan, where is our luggage?"

"It was Alex who was supposed to be getting it."

But Aunt Grace wasn't listening to him. She was already focused on Alex's recital of which aircraft were landing and how many there were from each airline company.

Ryan shook his head and walked back to the carousel. Sometimes he just could not believe how stupid his brother was. Ryan could see how Aunt Grace wouldn't understand. *She* wasn't Chinese. But Alex should know better. Some of these rules had been around for hundreds, maybe even thousands of years. Just wait until he told Uncle Peter about Alex wanting to get his hair cut. There's no way he'd let him. Where had Uncle Peter gone anyway?

Ryan looked around to see if he could catch sight of his uncle. He didn't see him, but he noticed a lion dancer, different from the other one. This lion had only one person inside the costume, and he seemed to be struggling to remove the heavy mask.

When the performer finally pulled free, Ryan saw that he was quite a big man. Big for a Chinese person. And he was dressed in odd clothes. Instead of a regular shirt and pants, he wore a long, shiny black tunic. His sleeves were so long, they hid his hands. The high collar was fastened tightly around his large neck.

Ryan saw Alex and Aunt Grace smiling and laughing under the arrival screen. They were probably laughing at him. He turned his back on them and watched the dragon dancer reach back and pull out a long, single black braid from inside his collar. The braid fell straight down the man's back, nearly reaching his waist. A queue? In this day and age?

The man stopped moving as if he sensed he was being watched. Ever so slowly, he turned just his head to face Ryan. A strange smile crept over his dark face.

The hair on the back of Ryan's neck stood up. He wanted to look away from the man's round, doll-like eyes, but he couldn't do it. When Ryan tried to blink, his eyelids stayed frozen wide.

From very far off, he heard, "Ryan, honey. Are you all right?"

He felt his aunt's hand on his arm and tried to turn toward her but felt frozen.

"Ryan!" his uncle said. "Chop, chop. I've got the trolley — and here comes your suitcase. Grab it before it goes around again."

Ryan couldn't move.

"Hey!" Ryan heard and saw Alex directly in front of him. Alex's face momentarily blocked out the man's hypnotic gaze. He waved his hands in front of Ryan. "What's with you?"

Ryan shut his burning eyes and pulled off his glasses. He felt like he did after running a long-distance race that he hadn't properly trained for. All of his energy was gone, siphoned out of him. As he rubbed his eyes, Ryan felt the gentle touch of Aunt Grace's hand on his head.

She said, "Are you okay, sweetheart?"

His face felt scorched, but he nodded. "Yeah. I don't know what happened. I was looking at a man over there," he said, pointing away from them. "He was one of the lion dancers."

"What man?" Alex asked.

"The one with the weird eyes," Ryan said as he put his glasses back on. He raised a hand over his forehead like a shield and looked to where the man had stood. There was no sign of him – or the costume.

He'd disappeared.

CHAPTER 7

Enter the Dragon

HONG MEI SLIPPED into the employee washroom at the Hong Kong airport and ducked into a stall. She removed the phony glasses from her face and pulled off the long wig. Holding it up before her, she thought it looked only a little shorter than her own hair used to be.

As she unbuttoned the passport clerk disguise, Hong Mei noticed again how perfectly it fit. She removed her own trousers and red turtleneck from the backpack Madam Ching had given her and pulled the clothes on. Then she reached back in and removed a black nylon jacket. She put it on and zipped it up. This, too, was the correct size.

She picked up the uniform, hairpiece and glasses and stuffed them into a plastic bag before unlocking the door and walking out of the stall. She moved quickly toward the garbage can and pushed the plastic bag into it. Then she unzipped the left pocket of her jacket and took out her new watch. The design on its round, white face was of a dragon and phoenix facing each other. Black Chinese characters representing the hours formed a circle running around the border. In the centre, between the two creatures' bodies, was a small rectangle. Inside this were red flashing numbers. The display beat like a pulse: 51:27:17

Fifty-one hours, twenty-seven minutes, and seventeen seconds. When Madam Ching had given Hong Mei the timepiece, the woman had said it acted like a timer, counting down the hours, minutes and seconds left until the Year of the Golden Dragon began.

There was just a little over two days before New Year's Eve.

For what seemed the umpteenth time, Hong Mei began to run through a mental checklist:

✔ Get a close look at the boys. (Done. They looked just like they did in the photographs given to her by Madam Ching.)

✔ Follow the Wongs and wait for Ryan and Alex to be alone.

✔ Convince them that their jade pendants really belong to Black Dragon and that because of what it says in an ancient scroll, they have to return to Beijing with me to give all of our jade to Madam Ching. Black Dragon will know his jade is being returned and will come to receive it. We will be able to capture him so that the world sees that Chinese dragons actually exist.

Right. How ridiculous. Those two boys were never going to believe her. They would probably think she was crazy, or worse, part of a kidnapping ring or something. They were probably much smarter than she was.

Beep! Beep! Beep!

The alarm sounded on her watch – a signal that the Wongs' luggage was being sent out. It was time to go to where the family would be waiting.

A woman was standing just outside the staff toilet. "Follow me," she said to Hong Mei. She unlocked a door upon which was marked *No Entry* and held it open for her, pointing toward one of the dozens of baggage carousels. "They are over there," she said.

Hong Mei spotted the Wong family, but she did not move. Her heart sped up when the woman nudged her forward and the door closed behind her.

She slipped her hand into her pocket. Gripping her jade, she walked slowly toward the luggage area.

Hong Mei saw Ryan, Alex and the foreign woman, their aunt. The younger boy and his aunt were talking while the older boy stared away from them at something. He stood motionless and unblinking, as if he had been turned to stone. Hong Mei followed Ryan's gaze and gasped. A man was staring at him with such intensity that the air between them appeared to vibrate. Hong Mei could feel the stranger's power from where she stood.

She watched as Alex approached his brother. Alex said something to the older boy, but Ryan didn't respond. Hong Mei saw Alex step directly in front of his sibling, waving his hands in the air. The energy between the man and older boy immediately disappeared. Ryan removed his glasses and rubbed his face.

The din and commotion in the giant hall suddenly

subsided. The sounds of hundreds of people became muffled as if a blanket had been dropped over them. Everyone still moved around her, but their actions were delayed and exaggerated.

What's happening?

Hong Mei glanced toward the man. Her instincts told her not to look directly at him, but her eyes were drawn to his. She tried to cast a charm of protection over herself, but for some reason Hong Mei couldn't remember it.

The man stared directly into her pupils. A second later, her eyes felt like they were being torn from their sockets. Hong Mei's mind fought the man. Her father had trained her well, and she knew her *gong fu* used to be excellent, but she was out of practice. She tried to imagine her own energy pushing the man's back at him, but all her strength and discipline had vanished. What kind of power was this?

Deep inside her head she heard, "It is old power – as ancient as the universe itself. Do not fight it, for it is part of you."

Snap!

Hong Mei was released with such force that her head flipped back, as if her neck was an elastic band. Her head rebounded and her chin smashed against her chest, snapping her teeth into her tongue. She tasted blood.

She looked down and cupped her shaking hands around her eyes like blinders. Once again, she could hear and see everyone in a normal way. People were laughing and talking, jostling to retrieve their suitcases and other luggage. Nobody seemed to have noticed what had just happened to her.

Hong Mei squinted towards where the Wong family was. They were gone.

Good!

She wanted to go, too. She didn't need this.

"Young Chen, I presume?" she heard someone hiss from behind, spitting something hot and wet onto the back of her neck. Her sense of the surroundings dulled once more.

"Yeow!" she screeched, turning around and striking a warrior's defence pose. Her body and brain were beginning to remember.

The strange man now stood grinning at her, inches away from her face. His eyes were hidden behind large, heavy sunglasses. Hong Mei felt her insides turn to water, but she held her stance.

"Ahhh, Chen," the man said. He breathed into her face and began to giggle. The sound was like a high-pitched squeal, twisting her eardrums and burning into her head. "This modern *gong fu* cannot protect Young Chen from Black Dragon."

Hong Mei recoiled from the stench of his breath. She tried to back up, but felt frozen in position. *Black Dragon?*

The man sneered. "Young Chen is very delicate."

Hong Mei glanced around for help. Surely there was someone who could –

The man breathed heavily as he began to circle around her. He was so near she could feel his clothes brush against hers. "No one is able to assist Young Chen, for no one is able to see Young Chen at this moment." He pushed his large, flat nose into her hair and sniffed. "Young Chen smells like ancient herbs," he whispered into her ear.

Hong Mei's skin crawled.

The man only chuckled, his open mouth giving off the putrid smell of an open sewer.

Trying to breathe only through her mouth, Hong Mei managed to speak. "I can see you are a man of great importance. May I ask your name, sir?"

The man smiled gleefully, showing his teeth, cracked and stained. "Indeed, you are a Chen." He rolled his head on his thick neck from one side to the other, stretching. The closure of his mandarin collar looked as if it was about to burst open. "Master Chen was also fond of flattery."

Master Chen?

"Master Chen was once a virtuous and true friend of Black Dragon," the man said, pushing the sunglasses up higher on his nose.

Hong Mei barely heard him as she stared at the man's fingers. The nails were so long and sharp that his fingers looked like talons.

"Is Young Chen listening to Black Dragon?" he asked, glancing briefly over the top of his glasses.

Hong Mei felt a jolt in the centre of her forehead. She thought she might vomit and quickly covered her mouth with both hands.

"Black Dragon is dreadfully sorry," the man said. "Black Dragon failed to remember that Young Chen is a mere girl."

Hong Mei tried to keep her emotions in check, but her face turned red, giving her away.

The man stopped laughing and his face suddenly twisted. As he ran a rough tongue over his cracked lips, he grabbed one of her arms and said, "Black Dragon's precious treasure is near. So near that Black Dragon can hear it calling."

Hong Mei's arm felt like it was on fire. It bubbled and burned inside Black Dragon's grasp.

"It is nearly time for Black Dragon and his beloved broken stone to come together once again. If Black Dragon were as selfish as humans, Black Dragon would simply *take* the jade back and forget the promises made in the past."

Promises? Hong Mei took huge gulps of air and imagined coolness racing through her body to where his talon-like fingers held on.

"But that is not how Black Dragon thinks. Black Dragon does not only think of Black Dragon. It is true that Black Dragon has acquired some nasty human traits over the centuries; one of them being restraint." He growled and let go of her arm.

Hong Mei looked down in horror to see the nylon jacket melted and her new sweater singed. She could see her skin showing through, raw and blistered.

"Black Dragon has waited more than two thousand years for this reunification. Black Dragon will *try* to resist the cries of his jade until the appointed hour.

"Farewell, then. No doubt Young Chen has seen enough of Black Dragon's power – for now."

Black Dragon turned and slunk away, unseen by the crowd.

Hong Mei gritted her teeth and focused all her energy on the burn. It was torture. She looked up to see a child staring at her sleeve. Hong Mei winced as she took her jacket off and draped it over her arm, hiding the festering blisters. She'd have to think of a healing spell later. Right now, she needed to catch up to Ryan and Alex. But how could she possibly know where they were going?

The crowd pushed in front, behind and on both sides of her. Everyone was moving in different directions. She strained to hear Mandarin in the voices of people passing by, but caught only a few words. All she could hear was Cantonese, and she couldn't understand that dialect.

And English? Hong Mei dreaded the thought of trying that out. She'd only ever spoken English during her lessons at school. Would anyone in Hong Kong understand her?

Hong Mei started to nibble on one of her fingernails. She noticed, but chewed anyway.

Did Madam Ching know about Black Dragon and how dangerous he was? Was this really *the* Black Dragon her father was so obsessed about? She had to focus on Madam Ching's plan.

A few metres away stood a massive wall of glass. Hong Mei made her way toward it, gaping at its unbelievable size. She felt someone bump her, hard enough that she nearly lost her footing. Hong Mei saw that it had been one of two young women walking together. Both of them were slim and wore stylish clothes. The slightly taller one glanced back over her shoulder at Hong Mei. She thought the stranger was about to apologize, but she merely flicked back her long, jet black hair and raised one eyebrow in disdain. Hong Mei heard her say something. It sounded like "country bumpkin."

Hong Mei sighed. Even perfect strangers made fun of her. She couldn't imagine asking anyone for help.

Turning back to the glass she looked out at the night. Madam Ching had told her to use the Chen clan's legendary skills. For anyone in the know those were, of course, *gong fu* and their inherited second sight. This, she realized, was why her father had trained her so hard. Had he known that she would feel so scared and alone? Why hadn't he warned her? She guessed he had and that was why they took him away. He'd been so worried he seemed crazy.

It had been a long time since she'd practiced, but she now concentrated on the special breathing Baba had shown her. Filling her lungs and stomach completely, she slowly contracted her torso, pushing all the air out. She imagined her mind clearing of all thoughts, making way for new images. Hong Mei closed her eyes and began to focus. The roots of her hair started to tingle and she felt the faint tickle on her neck. It was working! Shapes began to form in her mind's eye, but the vision was still unclear.

Inside her head, she saw streams of coloured lights rushing past. Vehicles honked and there was the smell of diesel and automobile exhaust. Were the Wongs in a car?

Yes. As usual. She saw more clearly as the vision unfolded. There were lights on the dashboard of a car. Then, she made out the image of a silk-tasselled lucky charm hanging from the driver's mirror. She heard the excited chatter of several people talking at once. Was it English? No, Chinglish – a combination of Chinese and English. Someone was trying to speak Cantonese. There was laughter. She saw a hand reach over and turn the knob on the radio. Canto-pop music drowned out the passengers' voices.

Next she saw blackness. Was it sky? Tall steel beams stretched high into the inky night and enormous steel cables draped from one towering post to another. Lights of other vehicles flashed and buzzed past intermittently.

Was it a bridge? Yes, that was it! The Wong family was on the suspension bridge she'd seen pictures of. The bridge linked the island where the airport was and the mainland.

Her eyes flew open. She'd try to catch up to them on that bridge. But what if she couldn't, then what?

Frantically looking around, she saw symbols for taxis, buses, ferries and the underground train. She'd only taken buses and trains, and those were between her village and Beijing. The Wongs were in a car. She'd never catch them by riding a bus or train. What should she do to get to the bridge where they were?

Hong Mei took a breath and made herself stop panicking. In a second she decided that it would be better to take a taxi and follow the same route they had taken. Her mind made up, Hong Mei raced in the direction of the taxi sign. It wouldn't take the family long to cross the bridge. Could she catch them before they got to the other side?

When she got to the taxi rank, she groaned at the long line of people. This was obviously no time to be polite, though. Throwing her shoulders back, she began nudging and bumping her way between people while trying not to let anything touch her burned arm. At the front of the line was a young couple holding hands.

What was she going to do? She couldn't just leap in front of them and steal their taxi.

It was time for some help from Mama's teachings. She mumbled a quick spell of love over the couple and they immediately began to kiss and grope one another. As the crowd of Chinese stared in disapproval, Hong Mei used the diversion to slip into their taxi.

"Where to?" the driver barked at her in Cantonese, frowning into his rear-view mirror.

She didn't understand him, but guessed. "The bridge," she said in Mandarin. "Please. Go fast. It is important.

Very important!"

He snorted, but began driving. "Of course *bridge*. Everyone must take bridge," he said, eyes darting at her reflection. "You look Chinese. Why you no speak Chinese?" he asked in English.

"Wo shuo Jungwen ba! Wo huei shuo Hua Yu," Hong Mei responded.

"You in Hong Kong now. We use Cantonese. If you no speak Cantonese, you must use English."

"Thank you," Hong Mei said. "Thank you for the advice."

Peering into the night at the other taxis, Hong Mei realized how unlikely it was that she would catch up to the Wongs. The bridge was huge and obviously very new. There were mostly red, green and blue taxis with a few other cars mixed in. How would she find the one vehicle carrying Alex and Ryan?

She closed her eyes and started taking the same deep breaths she'd tried in front of the glass wall. Hong Mei focused only on the rise and fall of her breath, trying to lengthen each one into the next. The pain in her arm began to recede. The pleasant tingling of her scalp and neck returned.

An image began to form in her mind. There were streets, narrow and crowded with people and vehicles. Above them flashed neon lights and blinking billboards of every colour, shape and size. Some ran up the sides of buildings, others blinked on and off in store windows. In the space above the sidewalk, higher than a double-decker bus, hung flashing neon signs in bright pink, yellow, red, blue, orange, green and white. Yes, if white could be whiter than white, it was when it was in neon, Hong Mei thought. She knew Nathan Road in Kowloon was famous for its neon lights. Were these streets of Kowloon that she was seeing in her head?

She continued breathing slowly and evenly, letting the gorgeous vision take over.

The leather smell of the inside of the taxi faded and was replaced with – sulphur? Yuck! Her body swayed and she imagined feeling a fine mist on her face. Light rain? The softness of the taxi seat disappeared and was replaced with a feeling of hard wooden slats. Was it a bench? She made out other people sitting around her.

Ah! It was a boat – a passenger ferry.

She saw signs written in both English and traditional Chinese. "Beware of Pickpockets" and "No Spitting."

She saw another sign. What did it say?

Star Ferry Corporation.

The Star Ferry! The boat that ferried people between Kowloon and Hong Kong Island. The Wongs must be headed towards the Star Ferry.

She opened her eyes and sat forward.

"The ferry terminal," she said in English. "Take me to the Star Ferry."

The taxi driver looked into his rear-view mirror and said, "Okay. Which side you want? Kowloon or Hong Kong?"

"I'm not sure." Hong Mei's eyes pricked and she bit her lip to stop it from quivering. "I only know I must go to the Star Ferry."

The driver frowned. "You only young girl. Why you alone? Where is your mother and father?"

"Oh, they couldn't come," Hong Mei lied. "I am here to surprise my cousins."

"Well," the driver said. "You lucky you not *my* daughter."

He gestured behind him to the seat pocket in front of Hong Mei. "You look at map. It show you Hong Kong Island, Kowloon, ferry and tunnel."

"There is a tunnel between Kowloon and Hong Kong?" Hong Mei asked as she opened the tourist map.

"Three tunnel!" the driver said. "But you say you go to Star Ferry. You no need tunnel."

Okay, Hong Mei thought. I don't need to use a tunnel, but I still have to figure out which Star Ferry terminal I should go to. She looked at the map and found the airport on Lantau Island. She ran her finger along the bridge they were just nearing the end of. It was connected to a smaller island and then the New Territories and Kowloon.

She saw the snaking lines of tunnels on the map and the letters, MTR. That made sense. Madam Ching said it was easy to get around on the Mass Transit Railway, or MTR as everyone called the subway.

Hong Mei looked above the area called The New Territories. To the north was the rest of China. And in the northern part of China was Beijing. She swallowed.

She was a long way from home.

Clearing her throat, Hong Mei said, "May I take this map?"

The driver shrugged. "It is for tourists. Take it."

After a moment he said, "If you my daughter, I tell you to telephone cousins. Surprise no good."

Hong Mei smiled. He was gruff, but kind.

"You are right. Surprises are not such great ideas."

Seeming satisfied, the taxi driver turned the radio on and filled the car with the twanging sounds of Chinese opera.

Would Ryan and Alex be at the ferry terminal? Is that why she imagined it? Or would they be going there only to take the boat across to Hong Kong Island, even further away?

CHAPTER 8

Fragrant Harbour

S HARK'S *FIN* SOUP?" Alex asked as he looked down into the steaming bowl of broth. He picked up a small white porcelain spoon and gingerly dipped the tip of it into the thick soup. "What happened to the rest of the shark?" he asked, putting his spoon back down without tasting anything.

Alex's relatives laughed, as they'd been doing since they left the airport more than an hour before. Uncle Peter's family had been there to pick them up, all except Nana and Yeye who met them at this restaurant instead. They wanted to save up their energy and not waste it by driving to the airport and back.

Winston, Alex's cousin, slurped his soup and said, "Just try a little bit. It's one of my favourites, and it's really expensive," he added.

Alex glanced beside him into the older cousin's bowl and saw that it was nearly empty.

"Do you want mine?" Alex whispered, looking over to make sure Uncle Peter hadn't heard. "Quick, I'll trade you."

Winston smiled and exchanged his empty bowl for Alex's.

"There's plenty more food coming," Winston said, taking a drink of his beer. "I'm sure there'll be something you like."

Alex took a gulp of Coke. He knew he shouldn't have another one since he'd had so many on the plane, but he was glad to have something *normal*. He looked over at Aunt Grace and wondered if she'd eaten anything yet. He'd only seen her drinking the jasmine tea she always had in Chinese restaurants. She said its floral scent reminded her of her grandmother's garden.

Aunt Grace noticed Alex watching her and winked at him. She looked down at her bowl of soup and rolled her eyes. Alex laughed. He motioned slightly with his chin toward the plate of sliced, black preserved eggs. Uncle Peter said the so-called hundred-year-old eggs were better than potato chips. Gross! Alex knew they weren't really a hundred years old, but they did kind of look like it.

He shifted his gaze to Ryan, sitting between their grandparents. Nana was pouring more soup into his brother's bowl as Yeye beamed. Alex wondered if they even cared that he was there too. Nana and Yeye had barely said "hello" to Alex when they got to the restaurant and nothing since then. But they treated Ryan like a little emperor.

"Wah!" Alex heard Winston exclaim.

A waiter wheeled a metal cart up to the table. Displayed on a platter was the entire body of a roasted duck, shiny and brown. The server turned the cart one way, then the other, so everyone could get a good look. The duck's long neck was stretched out and its head faced the diners. Eew! Alex quickly looked away.

When the waiter was satisfied that everyone had had a good look, he turned the trolley sharply back toward the kitchen. The movement caused the duck's head to flop around. Alex took a sip of his ice-cold Coke. Maybe it would calm his stomach.

"Mmm," said Alex's cousin. "Peking Duck! They always show it to you before taking it back to slice up and then make soup."

"More soup?" Alex asked weakly.

Winston laughed. "Yeah. While we're eating the meat, they'll use the rest of the body to make some soup for us. We'll eat it near the end of the meal."

"The *rest* of the body?" Alex whispered. "Even the head?"

"Of course, the head," Winston said. "You can't make soup without the head. But don't worry," he continued, deftly picking up a peanut with his chopsticks and popping it into his mouth, "they won't use the feet for the soup. They'll serve *those* with the meat."

Alex felt really queasy now. He looked toward Aunt Grace and saw her nose crinkle in disgust. He tried to grin back. What he wouldn't give for an egg roll right now.

The dinner in the noisy restaurant dragged on forever. By the time a plate heaped with sliced oranges arrived signalling the end of the meal, Alex was yawning.

It was nearly eleven o'clock when the family of fifteen made their way out of the restaurant and onto the sidewalk. Alex was surprised to see how busy it was. The narrow street was filled with trucks, taxis, double-decker buses and cars. He looked up at a small patch of sky between the towering apartments and office buildings. He couldn't see much, but felt a fine mist falling on his face.

"Everyone ready for some sightseeing?" Alex heard his Hong Kong aunt ask.

Now?

Winston's mother motioned for the family to follow her. "Everyone stay together now," she said. "We don't want to lose any of you!"

Alex groaned and tugged at Uncle Peter's sleeve. "I'm, like, really, really tired. Do we have to go?"

"Shh!" Uncle Peter said. "Of course we're going."

Alex dropped his head.

"I'm sorry, buddy," Uncle Peter said. He crouched down beside Alex while the others walked on ahead. "We're all a little tired. But everyone is so happy to see one another again. Let's not ruin it, hmm?"

Alex looked at his uncle for a moment, and then turned to stare past him at the backs of his grandparents. Each of them had an arm around Ryan, who was sandwiched between the elderly couple.

Uncle Peter followed Alex's eyes. He softened his voice and said, "It's tough being the second son. I know all about it." He pulled Alex's cap down even lower. "We'll have a great view of all the New Year's lights from the water."

Alex sighed. "Okay."

"Let's hurry," Uncle Peter said. "We don't want to get left behind, or we'll never find them again."

Alex nodded, then dodged past his uncle to catch up with Aunt Grace.

The clan stayed close together as they walked down

the gangplank toward the Star Ferry. They were the last group to get on board the crowded boat, and there weren't enough seats for everyone to sit together.

"That's all right," Uncle Peter said. "Boys! Why don't you go stand by the side of the boat? You'll get a good view from there, and Winston can point out the famous sights."

Alex didn't need to be told again. He dashed away from the rest of the group with Ryan and Winston sauntering behind. The blast of the ferry's horn sounded, and the boat began its ten-minute journey from Hong Kong Island to Kowloon. All three boys gripped the wet railing as the old vessel bobbed through the choppy water of the harbour. As the wind blew salty spray into their faces, they peered into the drizzly night.

After a minute Winston said, "Look back toward Hong Kong now. Pretty nice, huh?"

They saw hundreds of skyscrapers, spanning the length of Hong Kong Island. The buildings were so close to one another that they appeared joined together. Clouds hung low over the city, hiding the top floors of the tallest ones. Nearly all of them were lit with masses of multicoloured lights. Some had huge Chinese characters blinking "Happy New Year" or "Good Fortune." Other buildings came alive with magnificent gold dragons snaking down their sides, the creatures' scales lit by yellow bulbs, the eyes flashing deep red.

"Yeah, you're right. It is pretty," Alex said. "But this water is pretty stinky, don't you think?"

His cousin laughed. "Yes, I guess so. It's because of all the freighters and container ships. When I was a kid, it was clean enough for people to swim from the Hong Kong side to Kowloon. They used to have cross-harbour races. Wai-gong entered in them sometimes. I think he even won a trophy when he was young."

Alex thought about how old Yeye looked now. It was hard to imagine that he was once strong enough – or daring enough – to swim in this disgusting water.

He heard Winston ask, "You know what Hong Kong means, don't you?"

Ryan replied, "No."

"Fragrant Harbour."

They all laughed. Winston pointed toward the bow of the ferry. "We're nearly there."

As the ferry was docking, Winston continued his role as tour guide. "Do you two remember Kai Tak, the old airport? You must have flown in there last time, with your mom and dad."

"I remember that!" Alex said. "It was a wild landing strip, right? We were so close to the buildings, it was like our plane was barely squeezing through them."

Winston smiled. "Yeah, that's right."

"We could almost see what people were cooking for dinner," Alex said.

"You don't remember that," Ryan interrupted. "You're just repeating what Uncle Peter said."

Alex felt as if he'd been slapped. "I do so remember it," he said softly.

"How can you remember that, but nothing else?" Ryan asked, his voice getting louder.

Alex's mouth quivered as he looked into his brother's face. It was full of hatred. And sorrow.

"You can remember Hong Kong from when you were three," Ryan snapped, "but you can't remember how the fire started when you were two years older."

Alex's eyes welled up.

Ryan turned away.

Alex wondered if he would ever prove to Ryan that he hadn't started that horrible fire. Everyone, including the firefighters and the police investigators, had told Ryan that Alex was innocent. But how had he managed to escape while the rest of them were left inside? It was only luck that the firefighters got to Ryan in time. Ever since then, Ryan remained convinced that Alex was lying about that night. How could he have forgotten everything? Alex wished he knew.

Winston cleared his throat. "Okay. We've docked."

Alex waited until Ryan and Winston got off the ferry, then he followed them.

Winston, Alex and Ryan disembarked and stood amongst hundreds of other people at the Star Ferry Terminal. Alex thought it was interesting to be in a place where everyone around them looked like they did. He hardly saw anyone who didn't have jet black hair and almond-shaped eyes. So far, he'd only seen a few "foreigners," as his cousin called anyone who wasn't Chinese. And one of them was Aunt Grace.

"Do you think they'll know we're waiting here?" Alex heard Ryan ask.

"I'm sure they will," Winston said as he stood on tiptoes, peering back toward the exit. "But Wai-gong and Wai-po are pretty slow." After a minute or so, he said,

"Look, you two stay here, and I'll go back and make sure we haven't missed them. If they get here before I get back, just wait for me. I'll meet you right here."

"Okay," Ryan said. "Don't worry about us. We'll be fine."

Alex watched his cousin jostle his way through the sea of people. He shivered. It wasn't anywhere near zero, but the dampness made him feel really cold.

"I'm freezing!" he said to Ryan as he pulled his hood over his ball cap. "Aren't you cold?" He hated that he always had to make the first move after a fight, but he did it anyway.

"Not really," Ryan said as he withdrew a pair of gloves from his pockets.

Why did he have to dress that way? Alex wondered, eyeing his brother's navy-blue wool coat and black leather gloves. Was he *trying* to look thirty?

Suddenly Alex smelled something. Something familiar. Something good. He closed his eyes and sniffed at the air.

"What are you doing?" Ryan asked.

Alex opened his eyes. "Can't you smell it?" He craned his neck and looked around until he spotted the famous yellow sign. "There! I'm going to get a cheeseburger. I'll be right back."

Alex felt Ryan grab his arm, holding him back. "Alex! You can't just take off. We're supposed to wait here."

"I'll be, like, two minutes!" Alex said, shaking off Ryan's grip. Then he stopped. "You're not scared to be by yourself, are you?"

"Of course not," Ryan snorted. "I just don't want to get blamed if you get lost."

"Well, I need to eat something normal after that disgusting Chinese food. If you want to stay out of trouble, you'd better come with me. We're supposed to stick together when we travel, remember?"

"Well —"

"C'mon. I've got lots of Hong Kong dollars." Alex knew something that Ryan couldn't refuse. "I'll buy you a chocolate milkshake."

Ryan hesitated, but only for a second or two. "Oh, all right," he said. "But let's hurry. I don't want them to think we've been kidnapped or something."

And they left the spot where they were supposed to wait for their family.

CHAPTER 9

The Cousin Camouflage

HONG MEI WALKED BACK AND FORTH between the entrance and the exit of the Star Ferry in Kowloon. She had told herself that she would see the Wongs by 9:30, then 9:40, then 9:50. Now, it was past eleven o'clock and there was still no sign of them. She'd bitten her fingernails so short, two of them had started bleeding.

In between chanting healing words for her arm and fingers and pacing from one end of the terminal to the other, she would stand still. As people swept by, oblivious to her distress, Hong Mei tried over and over for new insights. She needed another vision, but nothing came.

Where were the Wong brothers?

Finally, at 11:30, Hong Mei's painfully long wait was up. She spotted Ryan and Alex. Her heart raced when she saw they were alone and walking together away from the ferry terminal. Where were they going? She moved quickly to follow them. There was no way she would lose them again.

They were only a few hundred metres from the Star

Ferry when she watched Ryan and Alex enter a McDonald's. Under normal circumstances, Hong Mei would jump at the chance to order some chicken nuggets and fries. She had a small stash of money she'd saved for when she went to Beijing and could stop at a McDonald's. But she wasn't in Beijing, and these were definitely not normal circumstances.

Hong Mei stood by the door to the street and watched Ryan and Alex leave the counter with their food. Ryan had a drink of some kind, but Alex looked as if he was starving. He wasn't halfway to the door before he'd torn the wrapper off his hamburger and taken a giant bite. Weren't they going to sit down? Did all foreigners eat this way?

Ryan and Alex walked toward where she waited. They were younger than she was, but they seemed so confident. According to Madam Ching, Ryan was nearly fifteen and Alex only twelve, but they acted as if they knew exactly what they were doing. They didn't look nervous at all to be in a huge city like Hong Kong.

Hong Mei was terrified, but she stopped herself from thinking about it.

As they got close, Hong Mei lost her nerve and quickly turned away. She could feel her heart in her throat.

Ryan, the older one, held the door open to the street and motioned for Alex to follow.

"Are you sure you don't want anything else?" she heard Ryan ask.

"No," Ryan said, taking a sip of his drink. "Just hurry up. You can eat that on the way."

Alex shrugged and took another bite. "What's the rush? It's not like they'd ditch us here in Kowloon."

Hong Mei clenched and unclenched her hands. These

two spoke so fast. She'd never spoken with native English speakers. All of her English teachers were Chinese. What if they hadn't taught her well enough? What if she hadn't listened properly? What if the boys didn't understand her?

Ryan walked out and let the door swing shut behind him. Alex crammed the rest of the hamburger into his mouth and tossed the wrapper into a garbage can. He pushed through the door with Hong Mei at his heels.

She was just about to speak when she heard, "Hey, dudes. Aunt Grace told me to look for you here."

Oh, no! Hong Mei watched in dismay as an older teenager strutted towards Ryan and Alex. He looked about nineteen or twenty. Who was *he?* What was he doing here? She stood off to the side but still close enough to hear what the two brothers and young man were saying.

"Wai-gong's not feeling so good, so everyone's gone back over to Hong Kong," Winston said. "They decided to catch the last ferry."

What? They'd been left on their own? wondered Hong Mei. How could she be so lucky?

A second later, her heart sank when Ryan asked, "What do you mean by the *last* ferry?" His voice was steady, but there was an edge to it.

"The Star Ferry runs only until midnight," said the young man nonchalantly.

"They *all* went back?" Ryan asked, his voice squeaking, "Even Aunt Grace and Uncle Peter?"

"Yes, but –" the young man started to say when he was interrupted.

"I told you we should have waited for them," Ryan snapped at Alex. "You and your stupid ideas!" he nearly shouted.

The young man looked from Ryan to Alex. "Relax. It's no problem! Wai-gong's old. It's normal for him to get tired. He'll be fine."

Hong Mei listened closely. He had said "Wai-gong" for grandfather. Ah, he was the boys' cousin.

"Besides," the young man coolly cocked one eyebrow at them. "I thought you guys might want to hang out in Kowloon for awhile."

Hong Mei held her breath as she watched Ryan frown. "It's getting kind of late, isn't it?"

"This is Hong Kong! C'mon. What would you guys like to do? Do you want to go shopping? What about karaoke? There are tons of karaoke bars around here."

"Karaoke?" Alex's face broke into a toothy grin. "We've got one of those machines at home!" He stopped smiling and his face grew serious. "But aren't karaoke bars for adults? Don't we have to be eighteen or something?"

"Nah," the young man said. "As long as you don't order alcohol I can take you in with me. There are a couple of places that I go to all the time. They'll let you guys in."

Hong Mei stuffed her hand into her pocket and felt for her jade. Why hadn't she talked to them in McDonald's? Just when she thought she'd got a break, she had to deal with this guy.

"How are we going to get back over to Hong Kong Island?" Ryan asked.

Winston shrugged. "We can take the MTR — the train — for another half-hour or so, or take a taxi. We could even stay in a hotel." He waved his hand vaguely in the air at the streets teeming with flashing neon lights. "There are plenty to choose from."

"Come on," Alex said to Ryan. "We'll be okay with Winston. It'll be cool!"

Ryan's eyes blazed at the younger boy. "You are so incredibly thoughtless," he said. "Yeye could be dying right now, and all you can think about is you."

"Nothing's wrong with Wai-gong," Winston interjected. "He was just overexcited. I promise you, he'll be fine." He pointed to a 7–11 shop a few steps away. "Look, you two decide what you want to do. I'm going to get something to drink."

Hong Mei watched the Winston-man disappear into the convenience store. She heard Ryan say to Alex, "As soon as Winston comes back, we'll get him to take us to Yeye's. Uncle Peter and Aunt Grace would *freak* if they knew we were even *thinking* of going to a bar."

Her knees shook as she stood watching the two brothers. It was now or never. Hong Mei took a giant breath and stepped toward them.

"Oh, I am so happy to find you!"

Both boys frowned at Hong Mei, then glanced around to see if she was really speaking to them. "Are you talking to us?" Ryan asked.

"Yes, I'm sorry. I am Lily. Your cousin."

"*Cousin?*" Ryan said, grabbing Alex's arm and backing up toward the convenience store. "We don't have a cousin named Lily."

Alex looked nervously over his shoulder.

"Yes! I am from Beijing," Hong Mei said. She was feeling way too hot. The new jacket she had bought was much heavier than the burnt one. She could feel tiny beads of sweat forming on her upper lip.

Ryan narrowed his eyes and studied her face.

Does he recognize me? This was not going well.

Hong Mei saw Winston inside the shop. He was coming toward the door. She needed to work fast or she was going to ruin this chance. Silently, she chanted an ancient memory charm.

> Look deep into your mind,
> bright new memories you will find.

Winston stepped out onto the sidewalk and took a swig of his beer. He looked at Hong Mei, then at Ryan and Alex. "Hey, who's your –"

Hong Mei quickly recited the chant again, her gaze focused on Winston. She held her breath.

After a few seconds Alex said, "Are you our cousin from Beijing?"

"Yes." Hong Mei said, looking back and forth between Ryan and Winston.

The two older boys slowly nodded their heads.

"Right," Winston murmured. "I'd nearly forgotten about you."

"I'm Lily," she said, allowing herself to breathe again.

Winston took a slow drink before saying, "So, what are you doing here?"

"Oh," Hong Mei stammered. She must not mess this up. Gripping her jade, she said slowly and deliberately, "We came to Hong Kong to celebrate with you. It was late and we could not find a hotel in Hong Kong, so we find – found – one here on Kowloon."

She swallowed and pointed toward some buildings. "Mama and Baba and I were sleeping when the parents of Winston called. I came to tell you. They said Ryan and Alex should stay at hotel with us."

"Stay with *you?*" Alex asked. "Why? We're with Winston."

"Yes." Hong Mei gave Winston's can of beer a long stare and said, "Your Uncle Peter and Aunt Grace said they did not want you going with Winston. They said it would be best if you come to our hotel."

Ryan shook his head slightly as if his head was heavy. "Well, I can see them not wanting us to go to any bars, but I think we should just go to Nana and Yeye's. Can't we just take the MTR or whatever it's called?"

"We are to…" Hong Mei stuttered, tripping over her words. Madam Ching's instructions had been very exact. She had to get them alone and tell them about the jade. Ryan stared hard at her. She steeled herself. "No, your aunt and uncle were happy to know my family is close to Star Ferry. Your aunt and uncle do not want you out after such a long trip."

She saw Alex roll his eyes and sigh. "They're worried about the jet lag thing," he said to Ryan.

Hong Mei cleared her throat and spoke very carefully. "Hotel is very close. Just there," she said, pointing to one of the many buildings surrounding them. "We have two rooms. We can telephone them when we get to hotel."

She could tell she nearly had them convinced.

"I know you are worried about your grandfather," she continued, facing Ryan. "You can telephone him. Okay?" She forced a smile to her lips.

Hong Mei wondered how she was going to get them to Beijing if she couldn't even get them to a hotel.

"Well," Ryan said slowly as he looked worriedly over at Winston, who was taking another giant gulp of beer.

A red taxi suddenly pulled up just beside where they stood. Three people about Winston's age jumped out.

"*Wei,* Win!" A young man said.

"*Wei!*" Winston exclaimed back, smiling widely at them. "What's going on?"

"We're going to karaoke. You coming?" the young man asked.

"Nah, I can't," Winston said, nodding toward Ryan, Alex and her. "My cousins are here. I've got to take care of them."

Hong Mei saw one of the girls run her fingers through her long wavy hair and pout at Winston. Hong Mei turned to see if Alex and Ryan had seen the same thing. Ryan obviously had since he turned to her and rolled his eyes before his expression turned into disappointment.

Hong Mei felt relieved, but sad for Ryan. She glanced at Alex. He seemed curious about the newcomers as he looked them up and down, but pretended not to. She watched as Ryan pulled his shoulders back and moved towards Winston.

Ryan said, "Look, Winston, I guess Alex and I better go with Lily. Alex's pretty tired. *You* know what I mean."

"Oh," Winston said, not even trying to hide the smile he flashed at the pouting girl. "Are you sure you don't mind?"

"No," Ryan said, shrugging. He turned to Alex and lowered his voice. "I guess we don't have much of a choice."

Hong Mei relaxed, but only a little bit.

A moment later, all seven of them started walking, with the older foursome in front. Hong Mei, Ryan and Alex followed behind them.

After only a few steps, Winston and his friends stopped at a small door. A few people were mingling about outside. Through the doorway was a narrow staircase leading down. The thump of music flowed up the staircase and through the concrete.

Winston looked over at Hong Mei. "Well, we'll see you there tomorrow then. You'll take good care of them, hey?"

"Oh, yes. Very good care."

CHAPTER 10

The Kowloon Conspiracy

RYAN WATCHED Winston disappear down the stairs into the karaoke club.

He felt weird.

One cousin, who he'd met only once before, had just left him alone with another cousin they'd met only a few minutes ago. Ryan kind of remembered a cousin who lived in Beijing. He thought that she was perhaps an only daughter, which wasn't surprising. He knew about China's one-child policy. But the *really* weird thing was that he wasn't worried. He didn't feel scared or nervous or anything. Somehow, he trusted her and he really had no idea why.

"Come," Lily said. "You must be tired."

Ryan turned towards her and saw that Alex was already standing beside Lily.

"Let's go this way." She pointed toward a narrow side street. "It's a shortcut to hotel."

"*The* hotel," Ryan said.

He watched her instantly turn red. "Sorry," he said. "I didn't mean to embarrass you."

"No," Lily said. "My English is very bad."

Ryan regretted correcting her. Why did he do that? She was only trying to be nice.

"No, it's not. Your English is good," Ryan said. "It's better than my Mandarin."

"You can speak Mandarin?" she asked. Ryan watched her face break into a smile.

"Yeah," Alex said. "His Mandarin is pretty good."

Now Ryan felt himself blush. "No, it's not. I can barely speak it at all. I only understand a few phrases and I can read a couple of characters."

"Maybe we can teach one another," Lily said.

"Yeah, sure," Ryan said, noticing her dark freckles and trendy haircut for the first time. He suddenly felt even stranger than before. They'd only just met, but somehow he got the feeling he'd met his cousin before. Maybe he'd seen her picture in a photo album back home.

The street was dark and quiet compared to the one with the nightclubs. They dodged mounds of plastic garbage bags and soggy cardboard boxes.

"I guess garbage men work extra hard this time of year, huh?" Ryan asked.

"Garbage men?" Lily asked.

"Yeah — the guys who collect the garbage — trash. Whatever you call it here."

"Oh, yes," Lily said. "We call it rubbish."

"And *we* call it garbage. And it looks like you guys have lots of it," Ryan said.

"It is because everyone is preparing for Lunar New

Year. Don't you also throw old things out to get ready?" she asked.

"No," Alex said, laughing a little. "Is that what everyone does here?"

Ryan watched Lily frown. "Don't Chinese do this in Canada?"

"Hey," Ryan said. "Alex is the least Chinese Chinese you'll ever meet. He doesn't like the food. He knows nothing about the culture. And he won't speak one word."

"That's such a lie!" Alex said, but he laughed harder now. "I know what this New Year is all about."

"Oh, yeah?" Ryan said, feeling himself smile. "Why don't you tell us, O Wise One?"

"It's like when the millennium and Year of the Dragon happen at the same time."

"And? What's the really important part?" Ryan asked.

Alex puffed out his chest and smacked his lips. "Well, my dears," he drawled, "they meet only once every three thousand years." He clasped his hands behind his back and strutted forward as if he were an old, pompous man. "And that, my minions, is why we are here in this mighty city of Kong – to celebrate this extraordinary event."

Ryan couldn't help but laugh at Alex. He could be very funny – sometimes.

"Plus the fact that our darling Aunt Grace loves shopping," Alex added.

Ryan was about to add something when he saw a red car coming their way.

"Hey, there's a taxi," Ryan said, waving for it to come over. "We'll get him to take us to Yeye's. Do you know their address, Lily?"

"No!" Lily said.

Ryan watched her wave the taxi *away*.

"What are you doing?" he said as he stepped in front of her.

"It will cost much money," she said.

"So what? Alex has money!"

Ryan continued to flag the taxi down. When it pulled up beside them, the driver leaned across to the passenger side and rolled down the window. He looked up and said something Ryan couldn't understand.

"*M'goi?*" Ryan asked the driver in Cantonese. "Could you please take us to Hong Kong –" but the man cut him off.

"*Aiyeeah!*" the driver said, shaking his head hard. "No go Hong Kong. Too late!" Then he rolled the window back up and sped off.

Ryan sighed loudly as he watched the red lights on the back of the vehicle fade as it drove up the street. He suddenly felt very, very tired.

"I know you must be – what is it called – 'jet-lagged'?" Lily asked. "Let us go to *the* hotel."

He could see she was trying to be helpful.

"Do you think your parents can take us to Nana and Yeye's first thing tomorrow morning?" Ryan asked.

"Yes. *Mei-you-wen-ti,*" Lily said softly.

Ryan smiled. *No problem* – that was one phrase he knew well.

Lily smiled back with a faint pink colouring her cheeks.

"Come on you guys. I'm getting cold," Alex said.

The lovely warm feeling inside Ryan vanished. He turned on his brother. "All you ever think about is *you*, Alex!"

Sometimes Ryan really hated his brother. And he didn't care if Uncle Peter thought the word was too strong.

Stomping ahead of Alex and Lily, Ryan continued the walk up the street alone.

CHAPTER 11

The End of the Jade's Slumber

HONG MEI KNOCKED ON Ryan and Alex's hotel room door. She had left them alone and pretended she was going to see if her parents were awake. After waiting a few minutes in the stairwell, long enough for them to think she'd actually gone to another room, she had come back. When Alex opened it, Hong Mei saw Ryan was standing at the window. He turned to look at her as she walked in. When he realized she was alone, she saw his face drop.

"I'm sorry," she said. "My parents are sleeping."

"Couldn't we go in quietly and use their phone? We won't wake them up."

"I'm sorry," Hong Mei said. "My father would be angry. I don't think it is a good idea."

"I guess we'll have to wait until morning then," Ryan said. He reached up with both hands and rubbed his temples with his fingertips.

"Yes," Hong Mei said, relieved that Ryan wasn't going to insist she wake up two people who didn't exist.

She wanted to change the subject. "Is the room okay?"

Ryan shrugged as he glanced around the small space. There were two narrow beds with a small night table pushed between them. Across the room, just beyond the foot of the beds, was a wobbly stand where the television sat. The only other piece of furniture was a stool, pushed into the corner of the room by the window.

"It's okay," Ryan said. "I wish it had a phone."

Motioning to the window, Alex said, "I guess your parents didn't book a room with a view, huh?"

Hong Mei wasn't entirely sure what a room with a view was, but she guessed it was one with a better sight than this one had. Outside the window was another large building just a few metres away. An alley was several stories below.

"No," Hong Mei said. "But we are lucky to have a room. Chinese New Year is a very busy time of year. And it's good that our room has a private toilet."

"Well," Ryan frowned as he sat on the bed, "Most hotel rooms do have a bathroom, you know."

Hong Mei blushed. She was glad Ryan wasn't looking at her. He'd taken off his shoes and placed them neatly beside the bed closest to the window. She'd watched him pull back the covers on one of the beds and now he was lying back with a pillow behind his head. He was still rubbing his head.

"I checked in the bathroom for a toothbrush," Ryan said. "There wasn't one."

Did he think she had one for him?

"There isn't any shampoo either," he added.

"Perhaps we can buy these things tomorrow," Hong Mei said.

"Why don't we just call housekeeping?" Alex offered. "They always have things like that."

Ryan said, "There isn't a phone, remember?"

"Oh, yeah." Alex tossed his jacket and ball cap down on the floor beside the other bed. "We can go down to the front desk and ask them in the morning. I'm sure you'll survive not brushing your teeth this once, Ryan," he said.

Hong Mei watched Alex plop down onto the bed, ignoring the look Ryan gave him.

"Are you tired?" Hong Mei asked.

"No," Ryan said, stifling a yawn and taking off his glasses. "I just have a headache. Have a seat," he said, motioning to the stool in the corner. "What time do you think we can go to Nana and Yeye's tomorrow?" he asked as he stretched out. He undid the top buttons of his shirt and rested his head on the pillow.

With Ryan's collar undone, Hong Mei could see a cord around his neck.

"What?" he asked when he caught her looking at him. "Did I spill something on my shirt?"

"No," she said. "I see you wear a necklace."

"It's not a *necklace*," Ryan said as he reached into his shirt to pull his jade out. He held it forward a bit for her to see. "It's a jade *pendant*. You're Chinese. You should know all about jade."

Hong Mei felt her heart skip a beat. The jade was in the shape of a small, open fan. It looked like hers. "What is carved on it?" Hong Mei whispered, trying to sound nonchalant.

"It's the top half of a dragon," Ryan said. "Alex's got one, too, with the head of a phoenix."

"May I see it?" Hong Mei asked Ryan as she reached a trembling hand in his direction.

"You mean, take it off and show you?" Alex asked. "No. Sorry, it's nothing personal. I just don't like to show it to too many people."

"I understand," Hong Mei said. "It must be very valuable – perhaps more valuable than you know."

Ryan left the top two buttons undone, but tucked his jade back into his shirt. He pushed on his forehead with the palm of his hand and narrowed his eyes at her. "You look a bit young to be a jade expert."

Hong Mei glanced over at Alex. He was curled on his side, already asleep. "It is only that I think I know where your jade comes from."

Ryan yawned. "Oh, yeah?"

"Yes, it looks like a part of the one that belonged to Black Dragon."

"Black Dragon, eh? We heard it was an emperor," Ryan said, closing his eyes.

"Yes, but before that time, the jade was Black Dragon's. It was a gift to him from Nu Wa, the Creation Goddess. He loved her very much."

"Oh, *that* Black Dragon. Yeah, we grew up with that story, too. Our dad translated the legend from an ancient scroll we had. Did your parents ever read that old poem to you? I guess your version would've been in Mandarin, huh?"

"Yes," said Hong Mei staring down at her feet. "My father made me memorize it, and he told me many stories of Black Dragon. Baba talked so much about Black Dragon that we thought he was a little crazy." When she said this, Hong Mei felt something pulling at her heartstrings.

"Look," Ryan said, stifling another yawn, "I've got a wicked headache. I get migraines when I get too tired."

"Your jade —" Hong Mei started to say.

Ryan interrupted her. "I don't want to talk about my jade, okay? It was my father's." His eyes closed for a moment. "Why don't we talk about you, Lily? Your name, for instance," he said, fighting to keep his eyes open. "Is it common for Chinese girls to have English names?"

"Well," she said, "many people have Chinese and English names. My Chinese name is Hong Mei; Chen Hong Mei."

"Your last name is Chen, not Wong?" Ryan asked.

Hong Mei watched Ryan's eyes close. "That is correct," she said. "I'm not a Wong, but our two families are still related — they have been for hundreds of years."

"I see," Ryan said, opening his eyes again and looking at her face. "So, Hong Mei, do many Chinese girls have freckles?"

"What?" Hong Mei asked. Oh, no! Did he recognize her?

"You're the second Chinese girl with freckles I've seen today. I didn't think it was that common." Ryan closed his eyes again and smiled. "Lucy Liu better not find out. That's her trademark. And she's gorgeous."

Hong Mei said nothing, hoping if she kept quiet Ryan would fall asleep. She felt herself blushing. Did he think Chinese girls with freckles were pretty?

Watching Ryan give in to sleep, Hong Mei thought about Madam Ching. She had been right about the boys not being able to fight off "jet lag."

Hong Mei saw Ryan's chest begin to slowly rise and fall. This part was going as planned.

After a few minutes Hong Mei said, "Ryan, are you still awake?"

No answer.

She relaxed and let her head lean against the wall. She would wait a little while longer. Just to make sure.

Hong Mei's eyes snapped open. She must not let herself sleep. She had work to do.

She studied the two brothers lying on their beds. Alex looked even younger when he was asleep. Ryan looked older – at least seventeen. Hong Mei stood up and glanced down at the flashing red symbols on her watch.

45:17:28

Forty-five hours, seventeen minutes and twenty-eight seconds before the start of the New Year. That's how much time they had to get to Beijing and lure Black Dragon there. She didn't want to be around when he came sniffing for his jade. And she wouldn't be. Her part in this whole thing would be over and she'd be with both Baba and Mama. That's what the numbers on her watch *really* meant to her – how long it was going to be before her family was reunited.

Madam Ching wouldn't expect the three of them to give Black Dragon their jade, would she? No. She just needed it to lure him to her. But it was strange that she planned to prove that Chinese dragons really did exist right when Black Dragon was due to – what had she said? – *expire?* She was going to have a dead dragon to show the world, not a live one. What good would that be?

And if Madam Ching didn't care whether he was dead or alive, why did the three of *them* have to do her dirty work? Just because an old scroll said so? Well, Madam Ching was in for a surprise. Her Black Dragon was more *man* than dragon.

At least, he looked that way. Hong Mei felt the rawness of her arm. A normal man couldn't have done that. She thought about his horrible eyes. Whatever he was, she didn't want to see him again. As soon as she, Ryan and Alex led Black Dragon to Madam Ching, Hong Mei would take them back home with her and Baba.

From inside her jacket pocket she pulled out a square wooden box. It was about the same size as one of the disc cases she used in computer class, only several times thicker. A parade of people had been carefully carved on its four sides. Some of the figures were shown skipping, juggling balls, performing cartwheels or balancing objects on top of thin poles. Others were playing musical instruments while Chinese lions and dragons danced in a line. Centred on the lid were two words: Black Dragon. Hong Mei opened the lid and breathed in the scent of sandalwood.

When Madam Ching had given her the box, the woman had said, "We found this container at an archaeological site. Although it's just a wooden box, it might be useful in proving the heirs' jade once belonged to Black Dragon."

Hong Mei had thought that a bit of a stretch. As *if* it would really prove anything. So she'd asked if she could take the scroll, too. The two things together might be better proof. Madam Ching had said no, she wanted to keep it in case there was any trouble.

The last thing the woman had told Hong Mei was that when that they did put their jade in the box as one piece, they might feel strange – lightheaded or even a bit nauseous. If this happened, they were to remove the jade immediately, divide it and wear the pieces separately again.

Hong Mei had wanted to know more about that, but the woman had waved her off, saying that if Hong Mei simply followed instructions, everything would be fine.

Hong Mei sighed as she stared at the dark cherry-coloured wooden container. It was all she had. Was it enough to convince Ryan and Alex to come with her?

Madam Ching's words came back. "It is your destiny, dear. It always has been."

Hong Mei supposed she could always use a spell again if she had trouble.

Reaching into her back pocket, Hong Mei removed a leather billfold. Instead of money, she took out a creased and worn piece of paper. Hong Mei opened it up and silently read the simplified characters Baba had written out for her. But she knew the poem by heart.

Hong Mei folded up the paper again, but instead of putting it back into her wallet, she tucked it into the box and closed the lid. Ryan had mentioned a scroll and a poem about Black Dragon. This would remind her to ask the boys about it when they woke up.

Hong Mei set the box on top of the television and reached into her trouser pocket. Strange. Her jade felt warm.

She took it out and looked at it. The stone seemed to be pulsating, like someone had put a miniature light inside.

Hong Mei looked over at Ryan. She could see a greenish glow from beneath his shirt. She moved quietly over to him and opened his collar gently with shaking hands. His pendant was also shining.

Hong Mei touched it lightly with her fingertip. It was warm like hers, not cool as jade normally was. Once she felt the stone, she had an overwhelming desire to take it. She'd had this feeling before – the night she'd first held Baba's jade.

She no longer cared if Ryan woke up. The only thing she could think about was taking the jade. She had to have it. Slowly and very, very carefully, Hong Mei removed Ryan's pendant from its cord. He didn't stir from his sleep.

Hong Mei held both pieces of the lovely stone in her hands. They were unbelievably beautiful, and so very warm.

What about Alex's?

She moved to him and saw the red cord lying against the skin of his neck. Her fingers were no longer trembling as she calmly lifted the thin rope. There was only a small portion of the green jade, but it, too, was shimmering. Hong Mei lifted the cord, undid the gold clasp and slipped Alex's pendant off. Even when she re-did the clasp and tucked the cord under his shirt again, he barely stirred.

She gazed at the three pieces of jade. They were an iridescent green, beating stronger and stronger in her fingers. She could only imagine how lovely it must have been when it was whole. If she put them together, the carving would look like the dragon and phoenix on her watch. The stones stirred in her hands. She had to see what it once looked like.

On the flattened palm of her left hand, Hong Mei fit each section to make an entire disc. It nearly covered the whole of her palm. The dragon and phoenix stared into each other's eyes as they must have so many centuries ago.

She had never seen anything so beautiful, yet so simple. It wasn't sparkly and dazzling. There were no stunning gems or intricately carved gold. The delicate etching of the dragon and phoenix was in perfect harmony with the subtle loveliness of the jade itself.

Hong Mei understood why Black Dragon wanted to have it again. How and when had it been broken? She wished she could see back in time and find out what had happened.

Hong Mei was so enthralled with her musings and the beauty of the jade that she did not feel the temperature around her drop. In a few seconds, the air was well below freezing. By the time she realized it, it was so cold she could see her breath. Her hands went numb and suddenly turned blue. She saw frost creeping over her body and clothes. Her trousers and jacket turned white and stiff.

The jade in her frozen palm was the colour of a lime Popsicle. She felt herself becoming lighter. Her feet and toes lifted off the floor as she floated up.

Down below her, Ryan and Alex were sleeping, oblivious to what was happening above them. An icy mist surrounded her, but they looked untouched. Though cold, the veil around her was gentle and soft, like a fluffy cloud.

Hong Mei struggled to make her body heavy and drop down. She worked harder, conjuring up her *gong fu* breathing skills, but it didn't help. Hong Mei felt the ceiling at the back of her head and along her spine and calves. Her teeth chattered as her body was enveloped in ice.

Hong Mei imagined that when she was completely frozen, she would fall down and finally wake the boys. She guessed it would be too late for them to help.

She was thinking about this when she heard a faraway sound. What was it? Her senses were dull. Wind? It was starting to sound like a loud sucking. Trying to concentrate on what she was hearing, Hong Mei felt her body pulled and stretched. She tried to think one last pleasant thought: Ryan and Alex sleeping peacefully.

The next moment, she was wrenched from the room, hard and fast. Hong Mei veered and careened through freezing darkness, where images and voices and rainbows of colour swooshed past. She gasped for air in the beautiful but horrifying void.

There was none, and she quickly lost consciousness.

CHAPTER 12

Escape from Black Dragon

EVEN BEFORE ALEX OPENED HIS EYES, he knew he wasn't in his own bed. This one was hard and narrow, and the covers felt too thin. Aunt Grace had gotten him a deluxe captain's bed with warm flannel sheets and the thickest duvet they could find. Alex loved that bed. He wished he was in it now.

Squinting over at Ryan, he saw that his brother was sleeping. His glasses were resting on his stomach where he must have put them before he'd fallen asleep.

Wow! They'd really zonked out.

Alex's first impulse was to go back to sleep. If Ryan wasn't awake yet, it mustn't be time to get up. He closed his eyes again.

A minute later he heard Ryan yawn and stretch. Alex opened his eyes and watched his brother search for his glasses, then frown when he found them. He put them on, sat up and looked around.

"Where's Lily?" Ryan asked, glancing over at Alex.

"With her parents? I don't know."

He watched Ryan put his shoes on and make his way to the bathroom.

"It's already past ten o'clock," Ryan said, checking his wristwatch. "C'mon, let's get going."

"I just woke up!" Alex whined.

"So did I, but I want to call Nana and Yeye."

"Go ahead."

"There's no phone. I need you to go down to the front desk and find out which room Lily is in."

"You go!" Alex snapped. "I'm not your slave."

Ryan pulled the cover off him. "The sooner we find Lily, the sooner we get breakfast. If we're lucky, Nana will have some of our favourite dumplings."

"That'd be *your* favourite," Alex grumbled, dragging the blanket on top of him again.

"Fine. I'll go," Ryan said. "Just make sure you're ready when I get back."

"Yeah, yeah," Alex said as he stuck a pillow over his head and tried to go back to sleep.

Not long afterwards, Alex heard a banging at the door. He stumbled across the tiny room and opened the door. As soon as he did, Ryan pushed past him. He looked frantic.

"What?" Alex asked. "What's wrong?"

"Have you seen a note or anything from Lily?"

"No, I was in bed. Why? What's going on?"

"Would you please get moving and help me…" Ryan started to say. He stopped when he saw something on the television set. "What's that?" he asked, pointing to the intricately carved wooden box.

"I don't know. It's a box. What's your deal?"

"The guy at the front desk didn't know what I was talking about. He'd never heard of Lily or her parents."

"Maybe you didn't get the name right."

"I got it right," Ryan said. He moved over to the TV and picked up the box. "Was this in the room when we got here?"

"I don't know," Alex said, turning the light on in the bathroom and closing the door. Ryan was asking way too many questions this early in the morning.

He turned on the tap and waited for the water to get warm. He pushed back his thick hair. No doubt about it, he definitely needed to get it cut. Just as he did every morning, he reached up to adjust the silk string holding his pendant. The silk cord was light, almost weightless. He pulled the collar of his T-shirt away from his neck and looked into the mirror. Only the cord was there. Where was his jade?

Alex opened the bathroom door and went back into the room. Ryan had opened the box and was looking at a piece of paper.

"Have you seen my jade?" Alex asked, pushing the covers back on the bed he'd slept in. Still nothing. He dropped to the floor and searched under and around the bed. He stood up again. "Ryan? I can't find my jade."

"What do you mean?"

"My jade. It's gone."

"You can't be serious," Ryan said, still holding the box in one hand and the piece of paper in the other.

Alex glanced at the front part of Ryan's shirt. "Do you have yours?" he asked quietly.

Ryan dropped the box and paper onto the bed and reached up to his throat with both hands. He grabbed at the cord. When Alex saw that nothing was on Ryan's either, he sat down hard on the bed. Alex watched his brother feeling inside his clothes; then, Ryan did the same thing Alex had just done. He pulled the bedclothes off and fell to the floor to look for his jade.

"Do you think Lily took them?" Alex asked, but not really wanting an answer.

"Maybe, but why would she do that?"

"To show her parents?"

"I told you. They said they didn't have Lily or her parents registered here."

Alex was sure he remembered — what? Actually, he couldn't remember anything about Lily.

He looked at Ryan kneeling beside his bed. His face was the colour of the sheet. Alex picked up the box. It was about the size of a CD case, but thicker.

"Do you think she left us this in exchange for our jade?"

Ryan didn't say anything as he picked up the piece of paper and focused on it. His hands were trembling.

Alex's eyes were burning. He waited, trying to hold back the tears. He knew not to talk to his brother right now.

The seconds dragged on until Ryan finally said, his voice quivering, "I recognize some of these characters. I think it might be the poem Papa used to recite to us."

Alex sniffled and wiped his nose with the back of his hand.

Ryan folded the paper and put it back in the container. "Stop crying," he said without emotion. "You're the one who got us into this mess."

Knock! Knock! Knock!

They froze.

"Maybe it's Lily," Alex whispered.

"Shh!" Ryan said, slapping his hand over Alex's mouth.

"It's the man from the front desk," Ryan said under his breath.

Knock! Knock! Knock!

This time the sound was louder and more urgent.

The two brothers remained still.

"Have it your way. I'm coming back with a key and the hotel manager," said the voice.

Alex watched Ryan tiptoe over and put his ear to the door. "What do we do?"

"Grab your stuff and the box," Ryan said. "Hurry! We've got to get out of here."

The boys dashed out, and raced to the door leading to the fire escape. They threw it open and ran down the stairs. When they got to the bottom of the stairwell, they pushed the metal handle down and the door swung wide. Ryan and Alex were pitched into a crowded, extremely narrow alley.

Ding! Ding! Ding! Ding! Ding!

An old man on a bicycle swerved to miss them. On the back of the bike was a bamboo pole holding ten or twelve ducks hanging by their feet. Resting on the handlebars was a metal basket on which a large wicker basket of eggs was balanced. The boys pressed back against the door, trying to stay out of the way.

Pushed up against the building, Alex asked, "Why didn't we just stay and ask the hotel manager for help?"

"What?" Ryan glared at Alex. Then a puzzled look replaced the frown on his face. "I – I don't know," Ryan stammered.

Alex slumped down and sat on his haunches.

"Let's try to find a policeman," Ryan said. He nodded at the box in Alex's hands. "We can show him that as evidence."

Alex nodded.

"Maybe Aunt Grace and Uncle Peter have reported us missing," Ryan said. His face softened and he added more gently, "They're probably looking for us right now."

Sometimes Ryan was a jerk, but right now Alex was happy to have him as a big brother.

They began walking down the alley. There were covered stalls on either side of the narrow lane. People were selling watches, handbags, ladies' underwear and children's clothes. Others offered tablecloths, socks, fruit, books, compact discs and every size of suitcase imaginable.

After a few moments, they came to the end of the stalls. They were now on a wide, busy sidewalk. Between them and the other side of Nathan Road were four lanes of traffic. There were people in every direction. Some loitered in front of shop windows and others rushed around. Music blared, hawkers called out their wares and there was the steady sound of car horns. Blasts of exhaust spewed out of taxis, motorbikes and double-decker buses, covering everything with a black film of diesel.

"Look," Alex said. "There's a phone booth. Let's see if we can call Yeye's place."

"Right," Ryan said, "but how do we get the number?"

"Call the operator," said Alex.

Ryan picked up the receiver and pushed 0.

He stood listening for a moment, then frowned. Ryan said, "Hello? My Cantonese is not very good. Can you speak English?"

Alex watched him listening again.

"I need a telephone number for my grandfather, Mr. Wong. He lives on Hong Kong Island. Could you please look it up for me?"

Another moment passed.

"I don't know," Ryan said. "I only know his English name." He groaned. "Please," he said, "you've got to help us. We're lost and we don't know what to do."

After a second or two, Ryan smiled. "Oh, that would be great." He nodded at Alex, whispering, "He's going to put us through to the Tourist Police." Then, into the receiver he said, "Thank you. Thank you so —"

Ryan stopped talking and looked over Alex's shoulder. His smile vanished.

What had Ryan seen? Alex peered back behind him. He didn't see anything except vehicles and pedestrians. When he looked back at Ryan, his brother's face looked strange. He was touching his left temple and seemed surprised. When he took his hand away, his fingers were smeared with blood.

"Ryan. You're bleeding!"

Alex turned to look across the street again. A man with large sunglasses was climbing over the guard rail. Without bothering to look left or right, he leapt over the barrier and into traffic. He ignored the cars and other vehicles as if they didn't exist, snaking his way toward them without harm.

How can he do that?

Ryan grabbed him and said, "Run!"

They ran together as best they could on the crowded sidewalk, Ryan looking frantically around all the time.

Alex turned around for a moment and saw the man with the sunglasses was following them. He had a horrible grin on his face.

"Who is that?" gasped Alex as Ryan pulled him toward a wide set of stairs in the middle of the sidewalk.

"The guy from the airport," Ryan said. "Quick! Down here!" They bounded down the steps two at a time.

There was a row of turnstiles at the bottom with people lined up in front of several machines. The boys watched as a woman pushed a card into a slot and a metal barrier turned, allowing her to walk through.

"We need a ticket!" Alex said, tugging at Ryan's sleeve and pulling him toward one of the ticket dispensers.

Ryan glanced behind them toward the stairs. His face blanched. "No time," he said, crouching down and crawling under a turnstile. "Follow me. There!" Ryan shouted, pointing at a packed subway train. "Hurry, Alex! We've got to get on board!"

Halfway across the platform, Alex heard a voice speaking in Cantonese over a loudspeaker. The announcement followed in English. *This train is about to depart. Mind the doors, please.* A horn sounded, and the steel doors began to close. A woman stood just inside the compartment the boys were racing toward. When she saw Alex and Ryan trying to catch the train, she jammed her umbrella between the closing doors. They automatically opened again, just long enough for the boys to squeeze through.

"Thank you!" they breathed.

The doors sealed tight, and the train began to move away.

Just outside the window, Alex saw the man. He had removed his sunglasses and was staring at the box Alex held gripped in his hand. The subway picked up speed. The last thing he saw was the man shaking his fists. His head was tilted back and his mouth was wide open. He looked like he was howling.

CHAPTER 13

Advice from an Ancient Advisor

HONG MEI LANDED WITH A THUD. She lay on her side, half-frozen. Her black hair stood on end, and her pretty freckled face was covered in frost. Just above her blue lips were beads of moisture. Gripped in her hands were all three pieces of jade, still perfectly joined together as one circular disc.

As she regained consciousness, Hong Mei tried to open her eyes, but they felt like they'd been glued shut. She attempted to move, but her body was too stiff. Was she paralyzed? Had her back or neck been broken? Her heart raced. Thankfully, she could feel that.

Hong Mei thought of her *gong fu* training and the age-old mantra of "mind over matter." She focused on what her senses told her and felt the warm kiss of the sun on her face. From above there was the cheerful, sweet twittering of birds. When she breathed in, she smelled rich soil and the woodsy scent of pine trees.

Her shoulder began to ache, but despite the throb, she was relieved.

After a few minutes, Hong Mei was able to move her arms, legs and feet. Although every single part of her body was waking up in pain, nothing felt broken.

When she could finally sit up, she once again tried to open her eyes. With a little effort, they came unstuck and she saw that she was outdoors. Off in the distance, she could see a town, or was it was a city? The buildings didn't seem tall enough for Kowloon or Hong Kong. She heard the birds again and the low whistle of the wind tickling the needles of the trees. There were no sounds of city life. No horns honking, people talking or lorries rushing along roads.

Hong Mei looked down at her raw hands, thawing in the wonderful warmth of the sun. The jade seemed to wink at her, dazzling in its pale beauty. Had the stone brought her here? Why? With tingling hands, she divided the jade where it had once been broken. It snapped apart easily.

Slowly, Hong Mei stood up in the clearing where she'd awoken. There was a dark and thickly wooded forest next to her. What was this place? It was quite lovely, but oddly quiet. She'd never been to a place where there weren't any people. Closing her eyes again, she tilted her face to catch more of the sun's healing rays. Unlike most Chinese, Mama always said that a little sunshine was good for a person's health. As it warmed her aching body, Hong Mei wondered if that old guy with Madam Ching was right about her freckles. Maybe they *were* from too much sun.

After only a second or two with her eyes closed, the familiar prickling began above her forehead and made its way over her scalp. The sensation lifted the roots of her hair, making its way to the top of her spine. She was about to have a vision.

From behind her closed eyelids, she saw a classic Chinese-style structure. It appeared to be a large building, but she couldn't tell since most of it was hidden behind a high brown-red wall. She could only make out the top section with its steep, yellow-tiled roof. Several small bronze dragons were fixed along the sharp edge of the rooftop. It reminded her of the Imperial Palace in Beijing.

The vision began to change as it focused in on two black iron doors in the wall. A pair of stone guardian lions sat on either side of the doorway, fiercely facing down intruders. Between the feet of the female statue sat her cub, while her mate on the right side of the door sat with one paw resting on a globe. The dog-like lions seemed to be watching her. This was different. It was like she was not just having a vision, but actually taking part in it.

The heavy doors silently swung inward and an old, white-haired man in a long, dark robe stepped out. The corners of his eyes crinkled as he walked toward her with a gentle smile. Hong Mei felt herself relax a bit. Somehow she knew there was nothing to fear from this man.

When he was in front of her, the man stopped and reached for her hands that still clasped the pieces of jade. Holding her closed fingers, he said in a deep, trombone-like voice, "Dearest child. Long have I waited for this day to arrive."

Who was this man? He seemed oddly familiar.

"We have not met before, but we are related – from a long way back," the robed figure said.

Master Chen?

Nodding, he tenderly opened her fingers and put the pieces of jade back together in her open left palm. When it was one complete disc again, it started shining electric green. "Ancient magic has brought you here. This enchanted stone has unearthly powers."

Hong Mei bowed her head in acknowledgement.

"You look much like my own daughter did at your age. She, too, was intuitive and brave."

"I am neither intuitive nor brave, honourable Grandfather," Hong Mei said, keeping her head lowered.

"Oh, but you are. Do not doubt your true self. Your father thinks your insight is the strongest part of your character."

"Baba? You've seen him?"

"Yes," Master Chen said quietly. "I have seen him many times and he continues to believe in you."

"But he always said I was weak! He despised me for being a girl and not a boy."

"That is not true. It was only his way of preparing you for your duty. He set about to make you resilient. Why do you think you were named Hong Mei? It was not only for the beauty of that red flower, but also because it continues to bloom even in frost and snow. Your father chose your name so that you, too, would remain strong, even during very difficult circumstances. There will be obstacles to overcome, Hong Mei, but you will endure."

The stone shimmered as if it agreed with the old man's words. Master Chen cupped Hong Mei's hands in his gnarled fingers. "Objects of beauty have always tempted humans, Hong Mei. This lovely pendant is proof of how far humans will go for their desires. You must fight these feelings and think only of returning this jade to Black Dragon."

Hong Mei lifted her face and peered into Master Chen's watery eyes. "To Black Dragon?"

"Yes, to Black Dragon. Listen well, Hong Mei. You must make certain that you and the heirs return the jade by midnight – just before the New Year begins. All three of you must meet Black Dragon at the river in the capital city."

"Pardon me, Grandfather. I am very confused. Madam Ching instructed me to bring the heirs and jade to *her,* in the capital city."

"*Ching?*" Master Chen's eyes widened.

"Yes, Madam Ching sent me to Hong Kong to meet the royal sons. She told me to bring them and their jade to her. She wants us to use our jade to bring Black Dragon to her."

Hong Mei felt the man's grip tighten.

"Do not trust the Ching woman. Treachery and evil make her heart beat. If she told you she wants Black Dragon, this is already a lie. The mighty beast would kill her and use Ching's bones for chopsticks if he so desired. No, she cannot want to draw Black Dragon close to her."

Hong Mei felt his hands stay tight as he stared past her.

"Unless…" he mused quietly. "Unless she's decided to end their feud." He thought about this for a moment, then said, "Impossible! There must be another reason a woman from that clan has surfaced again." He snorted. "It is obvious she is frightened by its dark reputation, or she would not have bothered to send for you and the heirs."

"Dark reputation, Grandfather?"

Focusing back on her, Master Chen continued, "The jade is a reliable judge of character. It brought you safely here, to where Black Dragon and I once lived. If the centre of your heart was not true, the jade would make you suffer, not guide you."

Hong Mei felt a wave of delight at his words, but immediately after, guilt returned. She wished she was as good as Master Chen seemed to think.

The old man seemed to read her thoughts. "Trust in yourself, Hong Mei, and remember that even with the jade's assistance, great caution is needed in your quest. It *must* be passed from you three heirs directly to Black Dragon. That is what was promised."

"But Grandfather, I met Black Dragon and he was terrifying." She felt a surge of pain run through her wounded arm.

"Do not fear Black Dragon, Granddaughter. He only wants his precious jade so that humans cannot misuse its powers after he is gone. Black Dragon gave up his chance at immortality for us. He asked only that we return his jade before he dies. We must respect this."

"Must we *give* Black Dragon our jade? Can we not just show it to him?"

"No!" Master Chen bellowed. His voice thundered across the ages. "You must not even think this way. The fate of our family and the Emperor's heirs lies with you. Since this Ching woman has emerged, perhaps even more people will be harmed. Your father told me of your visions and I fear they are not only images of our grisly past. They may be portents of an even more terrible future. Too many will die if the promise is not kept, just as they did so very long ago."

His voice became quiet again. "There is much to be learned from dragons, Hong Mei. It is so very sad that your generation will live without them. But your peers are fortunate to have you in their midst. You, with your gift of dragon's blood."

"*Dragon's* blood?"

"Of course," Master Chen said, his face smiling and frowning at the same time. "Did you not know? It was a gift from the creator goddess Nu Wa. To Black Dragon, she granted everlasting life. And to me, a young scholar and faithful friend of Black Dragon, she gave an infusion of dragon's blood. Over the generations, this has thinned, of course. But your ability, Granddaughter, to envision the past and the future, proves that you have traces of Nu Wa's legacy. Ah, child, you have much to learn before tomorrow night. I wish we had more time together."

Hong Mei's hands were released from his firm hold as mist began to swirl at their feet. Her heart sank as Master Chen began to fade. "Please, Grandfather. Don't go. I still have so many questions. Won't you please stay a little longer?" Her voice cracked. "Can't you stay and help me?"

"No, I cannot. It is your task to perform and it is you who must lead the heirs. Remember – listen to your instincts. Be strong and proud, Hong Mei, for you are the chosen one."

Master Chen walked back toward the door as the vapours grew thick between the two of them. He stopped and turned his head. "Use Black Dragon's treasure only when you need to, Granddaughter. It will take you where you wish to go, but each time you use the jade, you will become more dependent on it. It is very difficult to give back something so wonderful, is it not, my child?"

Even in her vision, Hong Mei felt herself blushing.

Master Chen stepped over the threshold and through the doorway. She heard him shout a few last words, "Let nothing stand in your way." The door closed and the building disappeared into the cloud and fog.

Hong Mei's vision ended and she was once again all alone.

She took a shaky breath and opened her eyes to the same clear, bright day she had awoken in earlier. A shiver ran through her body. She wanted to be strong, but she was so afraid.

Hong Mei looked at her watch. It blinked 35:26:13. Thirty-five and a half hours until New Year's Eve. The last time she'd checked was in the hotel room in Kowloon. Nearly ten hours had passed since then and she was hundreds of kilometres away. If she had ended up here, in the middle of China, where were Ryan and Alex? What must they have thought when they'd found out she'd disappeared – along with their jade?

Snap! Hong Mei heard a twig break.

The air whistled eerily through the trees. She thought she saw something move. Holding the jade pieces tightly in her hands, she felt herself being drawn toward the forest. As she got closer, she could see a break in the woods.

At the opening, Hong Mei peered in and caught sight of a large brown hare hopping along a trail. That's what she must have heard. Stepping onto the path and looking up, she could barely see the sky through the thick canopy. The strange quietness made her nervous. Hong Mei turned to go back, but found nothing but dense foliage. The opening was no longer there.

Still holding tightly to the jade pieces in her hands, she felt them growing warmer. There was a sudden flash of green light, like a bolt of lightning hitting the ground near her. She jumped and her body tensed, waiting for – what? Another icy journey? The flash quickly changed into a steady stream of fluorescent green light streaking down through the trees. Hong Mei thought of scary movies she'd seen.

A few seconds passed with no change to its intense light. Hong Mei realized she'd been holding her breath and let it out. Thankfully, she still felt the unchanging firmness of the ground beneath her feet.

Something on the ground where the light was focused caught her eye. It was difficult to see since it was also bright green, but she realized that it was a piece of jade. Although similar to Black Dragon's, the differences were its size and beauty. The disc was larger and it shone even more brightly than Black Dragon's jade had when it was whole. Could it be for her? Hong Mei's breathing quickened. Maybe it was to replace the one she'd have to give up!

She was about to step into the soft forest litter to take the jade when she stopped. Wait a minute. What had Master Chen said? *Objects of beauty have always tempted humans.*

Hong Mei gazed longingly down at the shimmering jade, admiring it from where she stood. "No, I can be strong. I can be stronger than I was before." Pulling her shoulders back, she turned away from the jade and began walking again.

For a while, Hong Mei felt good. She was confident and her body didn't hurt anymore. Even her singed arm was less sore now. Making her way along the forest path, she was almost beginning to enjoy herself. Everything around her smelled fresh and green. She walked on a soft carpet of pine needles, on and on.

Then Hong Mei's legs grew heavy and she started to glance often into the trees, sometimes imagining she'd heard or seen something. Ahead of her, the path stretched as far as she could see, with no end in sight. She was sick now of the smell of dirt and moss. They pressed in on her. She was thirsty. Really thirsty.

Hong Mei closed her eyes to concentrate. She heard a faint gurgle, soft, like a brook. Opening her eyes again, she followed the sound. When she thought she was near it, the gurgling suddenly stopped. Hong Mei held her breath and listened hard.

A moment later she heard it again, but this time farther away. She looked back and saw the path. Listening carefully, she followed the faint sound of running water. Again, just as she thought she was near, silence.

Thirsty and frustrated, Hong Mei stopped walking. She turned back toward the path, but could hardly see it anymore. It had grown darker, and she didn't know which way to go – to the trail or in search of water. She felt tears coming and hugged her arms to her chest. The pressure of these past two days overwhelmed her.

Why me?

The ground quivered beneath her and Master Chen's voice filled the air:

The fate of our family and the Emperor's heirs lies with you.

"I'm so thirsty," Hong Mei said.

The ground trembled again, harder.

Let nothing *stand in your way.*

Hong Mei brusquely wiped away her tears. "I am sorry, Grandfather. I understand."

She heard the water trickling again and this time could see the small stream, just next to her feet. Had it been there all along? Hong Mei stepped toward it and kneeled down. She didn't want to let go of the jade. Crouching forward, she lapped the water like a cat.

Once she'd had enough, Hong Mei stood again. Her head tingled and her chest started to feel tight. Had she drunk too much water or stood up too fast? A moment later, she realized that another vision was upon her. Her heart throbbed and beads of perspiration trickled down the sides of her face.

She heard panting coming from beside her and saw an image of Ryan and Alex, running hard. Their eyes were wide and filled with fear.

Chasing the boys was a man wearing sunglasses. The same terrible man who'd burned her arm at the airport. Black Dragon.

She heard Master Chen's voice:

I fear they are not only images of our grisly past. They may be portents of an even more terrible future. Too many will die if the promise is not kept, just as they did so very long ago.

Hong Mei saw Ryan and Alex now. They looked

terrified, but were no longer running. She watched the brothers, pressed in amongst a crowd of people, some seated and others standing, their bodies swaying in a gentle, rocking motion. Through metal-framed windows she caught glimpses of dark shadows flashing by. Then, through the glass, she could see the lights of a subway platform. The rhythm and soft jiggling slowed as the vehicle came to a halt. Some people near Ryan and Alex moved out of focus, while others moved in. But now there was no other sign of Black Dragon.

Hong Mei watched the boys sit down, wedging themselves between other passengers on a long metal seat. As her vision began to fade she could just make out that Alex was holding something on his lap – the wooden case for the jade. Black Dragon must have thought the jade was in the box! What would Black Dragon do if he found out the boys didn't have his precious treasure?

The jade. Did Ryan and Alex think she had *stolen* their pendants?

Hong Mei looked at her watch. More than an hour had passed since she had entered the woods.

She had to find Ryan and Alex and explain everything. The first thing was to get out of this forest and find a road into the town she had seen. Roads had taxis and buses. Maybe she'd be lucky enough to find one going straight to an airport. Even though Master Chen had told her not to trust Madam Ching, she'd have to at least phone her. No telling how furious she'd be.

Hoping for a bit of guidance, Hong Mei held tight the jade pieces in her hands. She squeezed her eyes closed and started thinking about Mama. And Baba.

Standing very still, Hong Mei thought of her parents. Baba had done his best to prepare her for this journey, and Mama had done what any mother would – she had tried to keep her daughter safe, even though it had cost her a husband.

Hong Mei felt her heart thumping inside her chest. She imagined each beat escaping from her body and rising up into the air. Maybe they'd land on wispy clouds and get carried to Mama and Baba. Then, like beads of fine mist, they'd slowly seep into her parents' bodies, finding their way into their hearts.

Hong Mei opened her eyes and looked around. She saw darkness at one end of the trail, and the unmistakable colour of blue sky at the other. She ran toward the light and whispered, "I can still hear you, ancient Grandfather. I will keep your promise."

CHAPTER 14

The Beijing Express

RYAN SAT STIFFLY on the edge of the metal subway seat. The train had just left the tenth station since they'd rushed to get on it in Kowloon. Ryan knew. He'd been counting the stops, wondering when they should get off. Worried that he and Alex would run into that disgusting man with the sunglasses, he'd convinced himself that they were safer on board this subway car.

"Where do you think we should get off?" Alex asked him.

"I don't know."

After a few more seconds, Alex asked, "Are you still mad at me?"

Ryan ignored him.

"I just asked what happened to your face," Alex said. "People don't just start bleeding for no reason."

Ryan tried to concentrate on the station names outside the windows as they approached each platform. He was hoping that one of them would sound familiar, or safe in some way. So far, he'd had no luck. "Can you just help me find a good place to get off?" he grumbled at Alex.

"A good place? How are we supposed to know a good place from a bad place?" Alex asked. After a moment, he said, "Maybe we should get off pretty soon, don't you think?"

"Uh huh." Ryan said.

"Fine," Alex sighed heavily, "whenever you're ready boss."

The train picked up speed and swayed gently back and forth as it whizzed underground. Once in awhile, Ryan could feel the carriage go around a curve, making a screeching sound as it scraped against the rails. The sound made him cringe. It reminded him of someone dragging their fingernails down a chalkboard. But that wasn't as bad as the thought of that horrible man. He couldn't forget the image of him howling when the subway left without him. And his smile, filled with cracked yellow teeth. They looked like fangs.

Alex shivered. Who was he? What did he want? Maybe he had escaped from a mental hospital.

Out of the corner of his eye, Ryan saw Alex tracing his finger over the carved figures on the Chinese box. He watched him open the lid and run his finger along the indentation in the shiny yellow silk lining inside.

"How does Papa's poem start again?" Alex asked, not looking up.

To take his mind off his thoughts, Ryan started reciting the poem with Alex. The two of them sat side by side, saying the words together:

Long before the universe was born,
Chaos rose from a celestial storm.
Alone for eons in an endless night,
The god awoke and created light.

Every time he heard or said this poem, Ryan thought of Papa. What would he have said about them losing their jade?

The poem was long and as they neared the end of it, Ryan began to feel better somehow.

Just as the words finished leaving their mouths, the train lurched hard: One, two, three times.

"Whoa!" Alex cried, gripping the wooden box and planting his sneakers on the floor. He grabbed the metal pole next to his seat to save himself from being thrown down, while Ryan, with nothing to hold, fell off the slippery seat and into the aisle.

"What was that?" Alex asked, staring down at Ryan.

He must be really afraid, Ryan thought. He's not even laughing at me for wiping out.

"I don't know," Ryan said, trying to keep his voice even. "Maybe we hit something on the tracks." He looked through the windows and saw that they were entering a station. "C'mon. I guess this is as good a place as any to get off."

Ryan stood up quickly and brushed himself off. Luckily the car was nearly empty. That fall had been pretty embarrassing.

The train stopped and the doors slid open. This time, the few passengers who were on board got off – but nobody got on.

They stepped out onto the platform and Ryan looked up at the two large Chinese characters painted in black on the wall. They were simplified characters, the kind he'd been taught in his Mandarin lessons. And he could read them.

It couldn't say what he thought it did, could it?

"What?" Alex said as he followed Ryan's gaze. "What's it say?"

Ryan swallowed. These two words were easy. One was "North" and the other "Capital." He'd learned them years ago. "That's just it," he said quietly. "What I *think* it says doesn't make any sense." He was getting a horrible feeling in the pit of his stomach.

"What do you *think* it says?"

"It says −" Ryan was interrupted by a man rushing toward them, blowing hard on the whistle stuck in his mouth. He was dressed in an olive green woollen coat, heavy black boots and flat officer's cap with a single red star above its brim. With one white-gloved hand, he waved Ryan and Alex away from the train. The other hand gripped a white baton that he pointed toward the escalator, directing the boys to join the passengers going up. Still blowing hard on the whistle, the man's face was turning purplish-red.

He pulled the whistle out and shouted, "*Zou-ba!*"

"Excuse me, but we don't −" Ryan started to say.

The man came within centimetres of them and said, "*Wo-ting-bu-dong.* This last stop!"

"Sheesh!" Alex said under his breath as they walked toward the escalator. "Keep your shorts on."

When the boys were on the escalator, Ryan turned back and saw the uniformed man staring at them.

"Talk about friendly and helpful," Alex said. "What did the sign say?"

"I think it said Beijing."

"Beijing, like the city Beijing? I don't think so," Alex said.

"Yeah," Ryan said as he thought of his Mandarin lessons. There was a map of China on the wall in his classroom. He'd looked at it at least a hundred times. Beijing was up near Mongolia. Close to Russia. It was thousands of kilometres from Hong Kong.

Moments later, as the escalator reached the top, the air suddenly got cold. Ryan shivered, but it wasn't just from the cold. Something – everything – felt different. They took a few tentative steps across the concrete floor.

There were hundreds of people getting on and off dozens of trains. Some rushed to get on board those which were about to depart, while others stood anxiously, waiting for friends and relatives to arrive. Many people carried babies and children, and even more struggled along the platforms with overstuffed suitcases and giant red–blue-and-white striped plastic bags.

He glanced up at the high steel rafters of the station's ceiling. They were surrounded by white puffs of steam and heavy black clouds of coal and diesel. This was a *real* train station, not a subway stop.

"Look," Alex said. "It's just a train station. We've been in subways before that ended up at a train station. Remember in London?"

Ryan put a hand on Alex's sleeve to stop him. "Shh! I know, but just listen for a second."

He watched as his brother cocked his head, paying

closer attention to the commotion around them. Ryan heard the steady drone of arrival and departure announcements over the loudspeakers. Conductors hollered for their passengers to board, and people chatted excitedly to one another. He saw realization seep into Alex's face.

They were surrounded by sounds and words they knew. There were whole sentences and snippets of conversations swirling around them that they could understand. Everyone was speaking Mandarin.

"Where are we?" Alex asked. The colour had all but drained from his face.

Ryan shook his head. "I don't know," he said, "but it's not Hong Kong and it's not Kowloon."

The boys huddled next to each other, trying to recognize a printed word or two from some of the signs. They peered at the heavy black strokes of Chinese writing. Ryan saw many of the same signs he'd seen downstairs on the platform. He gripped the collar of his coat and pulled it tight around his neck. "It says Beijing," he said.

"There's no way it can be the capital-of-China Beijing," Alex said shaking his head. "We were only on that train for half an hour."

"Pardon me," Ryan heard from behind him.

The sound of English startled them. He and Alex turned to see a young, well-dressed man. His jet black hair was cut short and spiky. He wore a dark wool coat that reached to his knees and at his neck was a cream-coloured silk scarf. His black trousers were precisely the right length, sitting on top of his shiny boots.

"Are you Ryan and Alexander Wong?" the man asked, showing off small white teeth.

Ryan and Alex backed away from him.

The man said, "Oh, how silly of me! I do apologize for not introducing myself," he said in clipped English. "I'm Ching Long." He thrust out a gloved hand for Ryan to shake.

Ryan looked at the man's hand but did not take it.

Ching Long offered his hand to Alex. He refused it as well.

"I am dreadfully sorry," he said, half smiling, half frowning. "Are you not Ryan and Alexander Wong?"

Ryan pulled Alex closer to him. He didn't want another Lily or Chen-whatever-her-name-was experience. Ignoring the man in front of them, Ryan held tightly to Alex while he looked around. There had to be a security guard or someone like that walking around.

He saw Ching Long frown as he too started eyeing the crowd around them. "Are you looking for Chen Hong Mei?"

Ryan turned to the man. He said slowly, "Chen Hong Mei? Do you mean Lily?"

The young man's face brightened again. "Yes. That is her English name. I must have forgotten that she would use that with you – but where is she?" he asked.

"We don't know, but we'd sure like to –" Alex started to say when Ryan interrupted him.

"Do you know how we can find her?" Ryan asked.

"No – I mean – yes," Ching Long stuttered. "I'm just surprised she's not with you. And you *are* rather early. We thought since you'd missed your flight, you might take the train." He frowned and looked questioningly at them. "My mother asked me to wait here for you, but I'm surprised to see you've arrived so *very* early. How did you manage to –"

"Look," Ryan said. "It's *really* important that we find Lily or Hong Mei or whatever her name is."

"Oh, absolutely," Ching Long said. "The three of you will most certainly be together. I am *quite* sure she will be there tonight."

"*Where* tonight?" Ryan asked, looking from Ching Long to Alex, then back to Ching Long again.

"Why, at the banquet," Ching Long said. "We're celebrating, of course!"

"Look," Ryan said to the man. "I don't know who you are or what you're talking about. We just want to find Hong Mei and get back to our aunt and uncle."

Ryan watched Ching Long's face lose its smile. The man looked from Ryan to Alex.

"Did Hong Mei not tell you about tonight?" Ching Long asked.

Ryan swallowed. He could feel Alex pressing against him. They shook their heads.

Ching Long whistled. "I see. Well, just to make certain, you are Ryan and Alexander Wong, I presume?"

"Yes," Alex said.

"Alex!" Ryan said. "Be quiet!"

"Please," said Ching Long. "Let me explain."

Ryan stared at him.

"Chen Hong Mei was to escort you to Beijing and to my mother's house," Ching Long continued.

"Okay, that's enough," Ryan said. "We're not supposed to be anywhere except with our family in Hong Kong. I have no idea how we managed to end up in

Beijing." Ryan grabbed Alex and said, "Come on, Alex. It's time we found the police."

"The police?" Ching Long gave a short laugh and said, "You are in China – not Canada."

Ryan and Alex started to walk away from the man but he followed them, saying, "What do you think *the police* are going to think? You are obviously Chinese – you are alone – you have no identification papers. They will think you are runaways or illegals."

Ryan stopped. "We'll tell them we're Canadian," he said. "I bet we have an embassy here."

"I am sure you do," said Ching Long. He nonchalantly brushed some lint from his lapel. "An embassy that's *closed* for at least a week, if not longer, for the New Year holidays. Where do you think they'll put you while you wait for your embassy to re-open?"

Ryan chewed on his lower lip.

"It will certainly not be a hotel," Ching Long said. "Have you ever seen a Chinese prison?"

"Who are you?" Ryan asked, feeling like he might pass out.

Ching Long's face changed and he smiled. "I don't mean to scare you. Things work very differently in this country. I only want to be of assistance."

Ryan looked at Alex, but neither of them said anything.

"Please. Come to my mother's house. If a mistake *has* been made, she will know what to do," Ching Long said.

"What do you think?" Ryan asked Alex quietly.

Ching Long didn't wait for Alex to answer. "As I said before, I am absolutely positive Hong Mei will be there tonight. Perhaps she is already at my mother's as we speak."

Ryan felt Alex watching him. He was desperate to get his jade back.

"Okay," Ryan said, "But I know our aunt and uncle are looking for us. As soon as I'm finished with Hong Mei, I'll take my chances at the police station."

"Fine," Ching Long said as he motioned for them to follow him. "My car is parked just over there."

Ryan and Alex walked together a few steps behind Ching Long. He called over his shoulder, "It's good that you are wary of strangers. These days, you can never tell!"

When they got to a black sedan, Ching Long opened the back door and said, "Please, get in!"

Once Ryan and Alex were inside, he slammed their door shut. They did not see him eye the crowd and whisper under his breath, "Yes. These days, you can never tell."

After sliding in behind the steering wheel, Ching Long closed his own door, started the engine and pulled away. The automatic lock button clicked shut.

CHAPTER 15

The Lethal Lady

AFTER LEAVING THE WOODS, Hong Mei thought she'd better get back to Hong Kong as quickly as she could. She found a road and a bus eventually came along. When she asked the driver how to get to the nearest airport, the man regarded her with suspicion and threw her a dark glance. Who knew what he really thought, but Hong Mei guessed that he considered her a teenaged runaway.

The bus ride revealed that Hong Mei was in Xian, of all places. Why had the jade sent her here? After a few kilometres, the bus came to an airport shuttle bus stop. Giving her one more dirty look, the bus driver told her the airport bus came every fifteen minutes. Hong Mei ignored the passengers' curious eyes and pretended she knew what she was doing as she got off the bus. Normally, she would have been embarrassed with so many people staring at her, but not now. She actually felt quite proud of herself. After all, she wasn't doing anything wrong. In fact, she was about to do something really, really right.

When she finally got on the airport bus, Hong Mei didn't pay any attention to the driver's or anyone else's stares. She was thinking only of what she needed to do when she got to the terminal. Although Master Chen had warned her about Madam Ching, Hong Mei wanted to call her and tell the woman the situation had changed. She would say that she and the heirs had missed the plane and wouldn't be in Beijing that afternoon as planned. Instead, they would arrive the following day.

Hong Mei believed this would give her time to get back to Hong Kong, find Ryan and Alex and secretly get them on a flight to Beijing without Madam Ching finding out. As promised long ago, the descendants of the Emperor and Master Chen would go to the river in the capital city and return all three pieces of jade by midnight. Black Dragon would take the lovely but dangerous jade, ensuring that humans were no longer tempted by its power. He would be able to die in peace. The plan seemed like a good one.

However, when she got to the terminal and phoned Madam Ching, the woman immediately started shrieking. "You Chens are all alike," she cried. "Did you think you could trick me? I suppose you wanted the jade for yourself, didn't you? I should have known a Chen would try and rob me of what is rightfully mine."

"I don't want the jade for my –"

"Silence!" Madam Ching shouted. "If you do not come immediately, I will have my people find you. Do you understand? They will find you and bring you to me."

Hong Mei swallowed.

"Are you there?" Madam Ching said.

"Yes."

"Bring me the jade, Hong Mei. I'm waiting for you," she said. "And so are the Emperor's heirs."

"What? Ryan and Alex? They're in Beijing?" Hong Mei asked. "But how did they —"

"Never mind how," she snapped. "They're here and they were found at the train station."

She cleared her throat and her tone sweetened. "It is just that we are so close, my dear. You must come quickly. We need your piece of jade to make everything work. We need it to draw Black Dragon back to his ancestral home, where he belongs."

"Black Dragon's home is with you?"

"Not with *me,* you stu —" She stopped and immediately returned to her cotton-candy voice. "Not with me, child. I meant Beijing. His home has always been the mighty river of the capital city."

Hong Mei knew the woman might be trying to trick her, but what she said made sense. Black Dragon would want to return to his own home to die. And Master Chen had said they were to give Black Dragon his jade at the river.

"Miss Chen?" Hong Mei heard through the telephone. "Are you still there?"

"Yes."

"Have I mentioned that I will be entertaining two other special guests here, besides the Emperor's heirs?"

Hong Mei definitely didn't like the tone of Madam Ching's voice. Even though it was carried over a long distance, it filled Hong Mei with dread.

"What's wrong?" Madam Ching asked. "Cat got your tongue?"

Hong Mei remembered Master Chen's words: *Treachery and evil make her heart beat.* "Mama and Baba?" she bleated into the receiver.

"I'm sorry," Madam Ching said. "The line isn't very good. I've got to go now, anyway, and prepare for my guests. Goodbye, Miss Chen. I hope to see you soon, dear."

There was a click on the other end.

"Hello? Madam Ching? Hello?" Hong Mei stared at the phone.

With trembling fingers she hung up and then quickly punched in her mother's telephone number. She let it ring twelve times before hanging up. When she closed her eyes and tried to conjure up an image, nothing came.

Were Mama and Baba and the boys really in Beijing? Or was it just a trap to get the jade?

After the telephone call, Hong Mei raced to the ticket counter where dozens of people jostled one another to reach the front of the line.

"Ouch!" Hong Mei yelped and pulled her foot away. "That hurt!"

Everyone seemed to want one thing – to get on the last flight to Beijing.

"Watch out!" Hong Mei snapped at someone when they dug an elbow into her ribs. She looked at the only ticket agent working at the counter. He sat unfazed, staring at his computer screen. All Hong Mei needed was one ticket. She'd even sit on the floor if they let her. There was absolutely no way she could miss this plane.

Hong Mei watched the agent stand up, yawn lazily and stretch. He ignored everyone in front of him. The crowd stopped surging forward and stared at him. With both hands, he combed his dark hair with his fingers, trying to cover his bald spot. All eyes were on him as he reached up and flicked a switch on the board above him. Everyone groaned when they saw the sign light up: *Flight Sold Out.*

Hong Mei stared at it in disbelief. She couldn't get stuck here. Who knew what would happen if she didn't get to Ryan and Alex in time? And what about her parents? She couldn't stand the thought of causing them any more trouble than she already had.

What was she going to do?

The ticket agent glanced her way and shrugged. "Sorry," he said pointing to the sign. "Too late."

"Please," she said, "it's very important that I get to Beijing tonight."

The agent ignored her, shut his computer down and left the booth.

"What do I do? What do I do? What do I do?" she said over and over to herself. In a daze, she moved away from the counter and looked toward the entrance for the gates. There were a few small shops selling souvenirs and snacks. She wandered towards them, the whole while whispering to herself, "What do I do?"

Surely they could squeeze one more person on board. Maybe if she went to the gate and pleaded with someone there. Perhaps one of the passengers wouldn't show up and she could take their place. Yes, it'd be better to be at the gate.

Walking past a jewellery store, she looked inside. Hong Mei's glance fell on a beautiful clock on a rosewood stand at the end of the jade counter. She went nearer and squinted. The hands pointed to 4:30. The plane was leaving at 5:00.

Hurry. I've got to hurry.

But the clock held her attention. It was lovely. Not the timepiece itself, but the delicately painted statue of the woman holding it. The figure stood half a metre tall and wore the traditional flowing robe of a Chinese goddess. She held the clock like a television game show hostess displaying a prize to the audience.

Hong Mei blinked. She'd thought this was the Goddess of Mercy, but it wasn't. It was Nu Wa, the Creation Goddess. Hong Mei moved closer to the statue. There were pamphlets and flyers splayed out on the counter next to the statue. Something told her to look more closely. She rifled through the glossy advertisements until she saw a plain white envelope. Snatching it up, she tore it open. Inside was a boarding pass for the flight to Beijing.

Looking at the gentle face of the statue, it seemed to smile at Hong Mei. "Thank you," she whispered. "Thank you, Goddess Nu Wa."

She turned and raced to the gate.

When she got there, she saw two uniformed men escorting a man off the plane. He was struggling between them, trying to get away from their grip. "This is ridiculous!" he shouted. "I *had* a boarding pass. How could my name suddenly disappear from the passenger list?"

The security guards continued marching the man away.

Hong Mei cringed, but she continued onto the plane and found her seat.

Now, buckled up, Hong Mei looked at her watch as

the plane's engine geared up. She saw the red numbers flashing, 31:57:37.

The aircraft began to shudder and roar as it picked up speed on the runway. Hong Mei felt herself being pulled back into her seat. This was only her second plane ride and it scared her. She thought about her parents; they had never been on an airplane. Were they at home now, or in Beijing? She tried to summon her second sight to find out. It hadn't worked since she'd seen Ryan and Alex running away from Black Dragon. Maybe she was too tired.

Hong Mei dug her hands into her jacket pockets and felt for the pieces of jade. How had the boys ended up at the train station in Beijing? Hong Mei felt dead tired, but she had to try. Closing her eyes she tried to get an image of the two brothers.

Blank.

She tried again.

Nothing.

A female voice spoke over the loudspeaker welcoming everyone on board. The flight attendant urged passengers to relax and enjoy the two-hour flight. They would arrive in Beijing just before seven o'clock.

Hong Mei's eyes remained closed, but this time it wasn't to use her second sight.

Exhausted, she'd fallen asleep.

"Miss?"

Hong Mei's eyelids stayed shut. She hoped whoever was talking would go away. Instead, she heard the voice again as someone shook her shoulder.

"Excuse me, Miss. We've arrived in Beijing."

Hong Mei forced her eyes open. "What?" she croaked.

The flight attendant gave Hong Mei a reproving look. "You must get off the plane. You are the last passenger."

Hong Mei remembered where she was and tried to get up, but the seat belt held her back. She blushed as she fumbled to release herself.

Hong Mei walked through the emptied jet and passed two airplane cleaning staff. She put her hands in her pockets and felt the jade pieces. Concentrating on the jade, Hong Mei missed the cleaners nodding to one another after she walked by.

Now that she was back in Beijing, what was she supposed to do? Would someone be at the airport to meet her or was she to hire a taxi and go to Madam Ching's place? Maybe Hong Mei should call first. There would be telephones in the terminal.

Looking up the ramp, she could see people rushing about inside the main building. As Hong Mei neared the exit out of the ramp, two large men suddenly blocked the doorway. They stood shoulder to shoulder and folded their arms over their chests.

"Miss Chen?" one asked. His eyes were hard.

Hong Mei's stomach somersaulted. She turned and headed back to the plane, hearing the men thumping down the ramp behind her. Just as she was about to get back on the plane, she nearly collided with the cleaners. Both of them were grinning at her. One held the back of a wheelchair, and the other had something in his hand.

Her breath caught when she saw it was a large syringe.

Were these the people Madam Ching threatened to send? Were they going to drug her and take the jade? There was no time to find out. The men and the needle were closing in on her, and there was only one way out.

Hong Mei yanked her hands out of her pockets to fit the three pieces of jade together. She was shaking so hard she had to grit her teeth and focus completely on the task. She saw the disc begin to glow. She squeezed her eyes shut, expecting an icy blast.

Instead, she felt strong hands pushing her down into the wheelchair. Then, instead of the sharp and sudden jab of a needle that she expected, she felt an unseen energy grip her skull. It squeezed hard, lifting her up out of the chair and turning her by her head. Faster and faster, she began to spin, as the force twisted her like a toy top. Just when she thought her body might fly apart, she was released and sent spinning into space.

CHAPTER 16

A Terrible Truth

WHEN CHING LONG had driven the car out of the hub of the train station, he told Ryan and Alex it would only be a few minutes to his family's home. Alex focused on the streets and any distinctive markings, memorizing how many lefts and rights they made in case they needed to get back to the train station by themselves.

At last they turned into a large tree-lined avenue with high brick walls. Alex thought it looked dreary in the grey winter afternoon, but it was probably pretty nice during the summer.

A few metres down the street, they turned into a driveway and stopped in front of a solid black iron gate. On either side of it were two tall pillars with an old-fashioned coach lamp on top of each. Ching Long stopped the car and rolled down his window to push a buzzer. A voice answered, and Ching Long called out his name. It was cold enough that Alex could see the man's breath.

A few moments later, a small, square peephole slid open on the gate, and two eyes stared out at them. Ching Long leaned out of his open window to show his face. The peephole was shut again and the gate creaked open, allowing the car to enter.

As they drove through, both Ryan and Alex turned to look out of the rear window. There were two burly men in heavy coats and gloves. Alex watched one close the gate as the other stared back at Alex with steely eyes.

"I wouldn't want to mess with those guys," Alex said to Ryan.

He turned back to the front and saw that Ching Long was looking at him in his rear-view mirror. "You don't have to worry about them," Ching Long said. "My mother has quite a large staff, but only five of them are for security."

"Five? Your mother must be a pretty important person if she needs five guards," Alex said. He was looking at the dozens of ceramic duck-egg pots lining both sides of the white gravel driveway. Inside each pot was a shrub with miniature oranges. He felt a tug at his heart. Aunt Grace loved it when these trees came out just before Chinese New Year. She always went to Chinatown and bought one or two for their house. He bit his bottom lip and stopped looking at them.

Ching Long broke Alex's thoughts of his aunt by saying, "My mother has married well. One of her ex-husbands is a VIP at CAAC. That's how she discovered you had missed the flight to Beijing. She had to pull a lot of strings to get those tickets, then when you didn't show up...well, let's just say she wasn't very pleased."

"CAAC?" Alex asked.

"It's China's largest airline company," Ching Long said with a sniff. He pulled the car up beside a wall with a large circular opening.

Alex leaned forward, "Is the VIP your father?"

"Mine? Oh, no," Ching Long said, turning off the car. "My father died years ago. I can hardly remember him," he added in a matter-of-fact way. He got out and opened the door nearest Ryan. He motioned toward the large round entrance and said, "Let's go through the moon gate, shall we?"

Ryan and Alex didn't move.

"After you," said Ching Long before he bowed slightly and waved them to go ahead.

Alex finally went first and stepped over the raised threshold into a large courtyard. There were a few pots of orange trees, but the rest of the space was empty. Across the cobblestones stood a plain brick building with a simple pair of wooden doors. On either side was a stone guardian lion. Alex remembered they were called *fu* dogs because they looked like a mix between a lion and a dog; a Pekingese dog, that is. Each of these statues had a bright red ribbon around its neck, like the ones the concrete lions at the entrance of Lions Gate Bridge wore at Christmas.

Ching Long nodded toward the double doors and said, "That's the entrance to the main house. My mother will be waiting for us in there." Once again, he motioned for Ryan and Alex to lead the way. "By the way, I hope you like cats. My mother takes in every stray that comes along."

Just as they approached the doors, one opened. Alex looked up to see a tall, slim woman holding a fluffy white

Persian cat. Its red collar was nearly hidden in its fur, but Alex noticed that the colour matched the long, high-collared crimson dress the woman wore. Her black hair was pulled high up on her head and was adorned with a string of pearls. She stood very straight. While stroking the cat in her arms, she gazed coolly down at Ryan and Alex.

"Mother," Ching Long said. "Allow me to introduce Ryan and Alexander Wong."

A thin smile appeared on her face as she said, "Welcome. I am Madam Ching."

Alex looked up at the woman's face in admiration. She was so very elegant. Alex knew that he should say "thank you" or something, but he couldn't speak. The longer he looked at her, the more he thought his first impression was wrong. She wasn't beautiful at all. Was it her eyes? They were pretty cold. And that smell. Sandalwood, wasn't it? He didn't like it, never had. It made him feel queasy.

Madam Ching's eyes remained fixed on him. Alex was starting to feel really unsteady.

"Ryan?" he said, moving closer to his brother. "I'm not feeling so great."

He saw his brother's face turn to his as a buzzing sound filled his head. Everything around him grew dark and he was having difficulty breathing.

He heard Ryan say, "Alex? Are you okay?"

The woman spoke. "Ching Long. Go get Lao Ming."

Alex woke up in a small windowless room. He was lying on his back in a single bed. There was another bed beside him and a nightstand between the two. A lamp was lit beside him and he could see another one on a dark wooden bureau on the other side of the room. Beside the bureau sat an old man. When he noticed Alex looking at him, he smiled and came over.

"Ah, good. Lao Ming wait for young master to wake up," the man said.

The way he spoke reminded Alex of Wai-gong, his other grandfather. He'd lived in Toronto for years, but still spoke English as if he'd just arrived in Canada. "I talk three kind Chinese, and little bit English," he would say. "Canada people lucky if they speak only one language."

Alex peered up at him and asked, "Where's my brother?"

"With Madam Ching."

Alex's stomach heaved. Just the mention of that woman's name made him feel sick. He groaned, but tried to sit up.

Lao Ming pushed him back down on the bed. Alex was surprised to feel how strong the old man was. He looked pretty feeble.

"Do not worry," Lao Ming said. "Lao Ming make sure no harm come to young Emperors."

Huh?

"Lao Ming sees young master has jade box."

Alex saw the man looking at the carved wooden box sitting on the table beside him.

"Jade is not in box," Lao Ming frowned, but in a kindly way. He looked very concerned. "Where is jade?"

"A girl who told us she was our cousin stole it," Alex said.

"Chen Hong Mei?"

"I don't know. She said her name was Lily. That's

why Ryan agreed to come here," he said as he reached for the box. "Ching Long told us that his mother —" Alex's stomach clenched again and he winced. Why was he reacting to Madam Ching this way?

"Now, now," the old man said, patting Alex's arm. "You are safe with Lao Ming. Madam Ching does not know Lao Ming is loyal to Chen family and Emperor's sons."

There was a knock at the door.

Lao Ming said quietly, "Shh. This our secret," then went to the door and unlocked it. Ryan and Madam Ching, this time with a kitten in her arms, entered the room.

As soon as Alex saw the woman, his head started pounding. He pulled the covers up and held them tight under his chin. He glanced at Ryan, whose face was blank and still, except for the little movements in his jaw. Alex could tell that his brother was grinding his teeth. He'd seen this expression of Ryan's many times before. Ryan wasn't scared. He was furious.

Barely looking at Alex, Madam Ching asked, "Feeling better now, are we?"

Alex's stomach gurgled as he watched the woman tickle the Siamese kitten under its chin.

Ryan came and stood next to him. "How are you feeling?" his older brother asked.

"Ryan," Alex whispered. "I want to get out of here. I feel really, really sick." A cold sweat was making him shiver.

Madam Ching moved to the other side of the room, looking completely unfazed. She opened a drawer in the bureau. "There are clean clothes for you here," she said.

Alex looked at Ryan, but he only shook his head for Alex to be quiet.

Madam Ching moved over to a wardrobe and opened its doors. "There are also more here," she said.

Alex saw several long-sleeved white shirts, a few pairs of trousers and two dark-coloured blazers hanging inside. They must be Ching Long's old clothes.

"Now then," Madam Ching said, "I will leave you in the capable hands of Lao Ming. Is there anything else you need?"

"Yes, there is," Ryan said. "We need to talk to Hong Mei. She's got our jade and we want it back."

Madam Ching's face contorted and her eyes grew enormous. She walked to Lao Ming and handed the kitten to him.

"*What* did you say?" she asked, moving quickly to Ryan and Alex.

"I tried to tell you before," Ryan said, backing away from Madam Ching, but still placing himself between her and Alex. "We want to see Hong Mei."

Alex hid behind Ryan, his teeth chattering. How could he have thought she was beautiful? She had the face of a witch. The woman looked like she wanted to tear Ryan up into little pieces.

"What?" Madam Ching hissed. "What did you say about the jade?"

"My brother and I usually wear jade pendants," Ryan said. "They were –"

"I know!" Madam Ching yelled. "Just tell me where they are. Don't you have them in there?" she asked, pointing with a long, red fingernail to the box that Alex held in his quivering hands.

"No," Ryan said.

Alex stared at the woman's hands. They were like claws. He had a flash of memory. Those hands with their long, red fingernails. He'd seen them before. He'd seen them holding a lighter.

Alex screamed just as Madam Ching lunged forward and snatched the box out of his hands. She snapped the lid open. When she saw there was nothing in the box, she threw it across the room.

"Where is it?" her voice was shrill. "Are you wearing it?" She reached for Ryan's collar.

He moved away. "We don't have it, okay? Hong Mei stole our jade."

Alex was shaking so uncontrollably he thought he would explode.

Lao Ming came to stand between the boys and Madam Ching. He lowered his head and spoke to her in Mandarin.

Alex held his breath and watched Madam Ching thinking.

Finally, her voice velvety again, she said, "*Xiexie*, Lao Ming. You are always so helpful. I know I can leave this with you, for *I* must find out what has happened to our Miss Chen.

"Make sure they dress appropriately for the banquet, won't you? I especially want them to wear the cashmere jackets I had made. We might not have the jade with us tonight, but my financiers are still expecting to dine with the Emperor's heirs." At this she smoothed her shiny red dress and took the kitten back from the old man. She kissed the top of the little cat's head before smiling tightly at Ryan and Alex. "You won't give Lao Ming any trouble, will you? It's not a good idea to upset a Shao Lin *gong fu* master."

Madam Ching laughed as she walked out.

As soon as she'd gone, Alex let his breath out and said, "Ryan! It was her. I *saw* her." Alex's heart pounded and he felt the tears welling up in his eyes. "She's the one I couldn't remember. She's the one who started the fire!"

Ryan's face went deathly white. Alex watched his brother stare back at him.

"Are you sure? How can that be?" Ryan whispered.

"I don't know, but I swear I remember."

They both turned to Lao Ming. He nodded and said, "I am sorry. What the young master say is true."

Ryan sat silently with Alex for a long time. Nobody said anything until Lao Ming gently urged them to get ready for the banquet. The old man said it would anger Madam Ching if they were late.

Just after seven o'clock, Ryan and Alex waited outside the entrance of the dining room, guarded by two large men. Before leaving them to check the food, Lao Ming had stopped them at the door and inspected the brothers again. Just when he was about to nod his approval, he caught sight of the peppermint in Ryan's mouth.

"*Bu-bu-bu!* No, no, no!" the man said, shaking a finger at Ryan. "Not nice to eat before dinner." He held his palm out, just under Ryan's chin, and said, "Give to Lao Ming."

Alex watched as Ryan kept his mouth clamped shut.

"Give!" the old man said. "Young Emperors do not eat sweets."

Ryan pushed the mint out with his tongue and let it drop into Lao Ming's hand.

Wow. Ryan had actually listened to the old guy.

While they stood in the doorway, Alex saw a big round table in the centre of the room, where a dozen or so adults were seated.

Madam Ching glided toward them. Alex instinctively moved back toward the door.

"*Qing-jin-lai*. Please," Madam Ching said. "Come in."

Ryan and Alex cringed and looked at one another. They knew they had no choice.

As the brothers moved toward the table, Madam Ching raised her voice and said, "Introducing Ryan and Alexander Wong – heirs to the Imperial throne and keepers of Black Dragon's jade!"

CHAPTER 17

Friends and Foes

CRASH!

Hong Mei fell hard against a wall.

Quack! Quack! Quack!

She felt the beating of wings all around her. Covering her head with her arms, she scrunched herself into a ball.

Things calmed down after a few moments and Hong Mei peeked out. It was smelly and dark. *Where am I now?* The light from the jade had dimmed. She broke the disc apart and put the pieces back into her pockets.

"Ow!" Hong Mei whispered loudly. Something had pecked her burned arm. "Shoo!" she said as she edged along the wooden wall towards a door. *A duck pen?*

"There, there," she said to the beady-eyed fowl watching her. "I'll just let myself out." She fiddled with the door handle and managed to turn it. She backed out into the night.

Hong Mei closed the door and surveyed the courtyard, catching a glimpse of a cat slinking along one wall. There were voices coming from the building next to her. She crept towards the open windows and crouched there, listening to the sounds of people working inside. Hong Mei stretched up onto her toes and looked.

In a large kitchen, several cooks dressed in white aprons and caps prepared food. Two people chopped onions and diced vegetables, while another two stir-fried in large woks. Wonderful aromas drifted out, straight up her nose. Hong Mei's mouth began to water and her stomach growled.

A man in a white shirt and black vest and trousers set a large soup tureen onto a trolley. He pushed the cart toward a swinging door and Hong Mei caught a glimpse of a dining room on the other side.

Something brushed against her leg and she jumped. Looking down, she saw it was a black-and-white cat. It peered up at her with big green eyes and meowed.

"Scat!" Hong Mei hissed. This was no time to make friends. Bending over again to move away from the window, she saw two more cats sitting by the kitchen door. They paid no attention to her but stayed focused on the action inside. Hong Mei looked up at the wall surrounding the courtyard. An orange tabby was strolling along the top of it. Wherever she was, the people who lived here sure liked animals.

She scurried along the brick building to the dining room. The room's windows were closed against the cold night air but she could hear a woman speaking.

Madam Ching? Hong Mei wanted to look inside the room, but she was scared. Would Hong Mei be welcomed for bringing the jade – or would Madam Ching attack her, like those brutes at the airport?

Hong Mei tried to make out what was going on.

Nobody was talking now, and she heard the scraping of chairs and shuffling of feet. Cautiously, she raised her head to look in the window.

There was a round table in the middle of the room. Ten or twelve elderly people stood around it, but they were looking toward the door. *At what?*

Hong Mei caught sight of Madam Ching and was about to duck down again when she saw two boys. Ryan and Alex! Hong Mei watched as the brothers moved to the table and everyone took their seats.

They're all right, she sighed. But where were her parents? She couldn't see them.

Her insides rumbled again. It smelled so good. She wondered if she could sneak something out of the kitchen. Hong Mei crept towards the door, drawn by her hunger. The two cats were still there, but this time they looked towards her and suddenly darted away.

Hearing a sound from behind her, Hong Mei was about to turn around when someone grabbed her. She opened her mouth to scream, but a hand clamped down over it. When she tried a *gong fu* move to release herself, she felt the grip tighten as her assailant dragged her across the courtyard.

Hong Mei went limp, trying to make her body heavy and awkward to carry. It didn't help. The person was incredibly strong. They came to a gate in the wall where she felt herself being pulled unceremoniously over the threshold. She was dragged a few more metres to a door in a small, windowless building. They stopped, but the hand stayed on her mouth.

"You must not speak until we are inside this room,"

a male voice said quietly. He spoke impeccable Mandarin, but his accent was unfamiliar. Hong Mei thought he must be from another part of China. "I will not hurt you," he said. "I am a friend of your father's."

Hong Mei tried to say, "Baba?" but the man pressed her mouth harder.

"You do not listen. Be silent or I will have to gag you."

Hong Mei swallowed and nodded.

He removed his hand, but he still gripped her tight with his other one. The old, bald-headed man opened the door and pushed her into the dim interior. Once they were both inside, he closed the door and locked it.

"Are my mother and father here?" Hong Mei asked, forgetting to keep her voice low.

The man clamped his hand across her mouth again. "I am helping you out of loyalty to your father. If I get found out, I will be killed. *Do* you understand?"

Hong Mei nodded again, more slowly.

"Let us try this again," he said while removing his hand.

Hong Mei took a big breath, but stayed silent, waiting for the man to speak. The skin on the man's face and hands were filled with lines, but his body looked taut and tough. She wondered who he was and how he fit in with Madam Ching.

"I am Lao Ming. When your father was young, I was his master at the monastery. It was there that he learned Shao Lin-style *gong fu*. And it is there that he has been staying, away from the authorities, but more importantly, away from Madam Ching.

"I have worked with Madam Ching for many years.

I understand the way this woman thinks, and she is very dangerous. There is nothing that she will not do to get what she desires. And what she wants more than anything is Black Dragon's jade. Did you know that she is the one who set the fire that killed the parents of the Emperor's heirs?"

Hong Mei didn't know this. She knew the boys lived with their aunt and uncle but she had no idea it was because their parents had been killed.

"After years of searching for the separated jade pieces, Madam Ching discovered they were worn by the two brothers in Canada. She and two or three of her henchmen went there to steal the jade. By then, she'd decided to eliminate any chance of them reclaiming what was, until the Year of the Golden Dragon, rightfully theirs.

"Her plan was to set the fire in the parents' room so there'd be no chance they could save their children. Then, she would take the boys' jade and lock them inside the house. However, everything went wrong about halfway through. The youngest one woke up and saw Madam Ching. Apparently he screamed so loudly the neighbour's dogs started barking, so she fled.

"Madam Ching decided that it was an omen. She would wait and draw up a better plan; one where she could use the scroll she had found in the boys' house and taken with her.

"She referred to the scroll and its legend as 'proof' for the existence of the jade and Black Dragon. She told her financial backers that their investment in 'The Dragon Project,' as she calls it, would earn them millions of *yuan*. She convinced them that a dragon, dead or alive, would attract thousands of tourists, foreign and Chinese.

Of course this was just a ploy. She only wants you to lure Black Dragon to her so that she may bargain with him. Though why she gathers you here puzzles me. The prophecy…"

But Hong Mei had stopped listening at the word *bargain*. "Please," she whispered. "May I say something?"

"You may speak quietly, but remember that we are in grave danger."

"I understand the jade has very special powers…" and she briefly told him about the two times she had used it. He listened with interest, but didn't look surprised.

"You, young Chen, were very fortunate with Madam's men at the airport. They are all thugs. I am quite sure you would never have woken up again."

"Is it this power that Madam Ching wants so much? So much that she is willing to kill for it?"

"Oh, it is not just what the jade can do. In fact, she is afraid of its power. She believes in the stories of people dying with it around their necks. That is why she has used you three heirs to bring her the jade, just in case there is any truth to it."

"To what?"

"She believes that the jade, if handled by someone who is not *always* honest, can bring bad luck, even death. One of the wives of an ancient emperor died with it around her neck."

"But Ryan, Alex and I are fine and we wear it."

"Yes, but that is because young people are pure at heart. Madam Ching is not and she knows this. *And* she is deeply superstitious. She doesn't want to take any chances, not after she was nearly caught in Canada.

"That is why she decided to act according to what was written in the scroll. She would go so far as to allow you three to get close to Black Dragon at the appointed hour. Just when you are about to hand over the jade, she will move in and make her deal with Black Dragon."

"What kind of –" But Hong Mei didn't have a chance to finish. She was interrupted by a deep sound of a gong coming from one of the courtyards.

"That is for me," Lao Ming said. "It's time to go and bring the young masters back here. In case someone follows me, you had better hide somewhere in this room."

Hong Mei nodded in agreement and said, "Lao Ming? Do you know where my mother and father are?"

For the first time, the old man smiled. "Yes, they are safe and together."

Hong Mei thought she would cry with relief.

"I must go and bring the brothers back here. After that I will bring you something to eat."

"Thank you," she whispered.

"Oh," Lao Ming said. "Do not forget to tell the heirs about Master Chen's box."

"What? What box?"

"The one they came with," he said looking annoyed. "Your grandfather's box also has great power. How do you think they got here?"

The gong sounded again. "We can talk about this when I bring your food."

Hong Mei watched the old man go out. She noticed he didn't bother locking the door.

Her head spun with what Lao Ming had told her. *Master Chen's* box? She had thought it was Black Dragon's.

Why had Madam Ching given her a magic box? Why hadn't she kept it for herself? And what kind of deal did she want to make with Black Dragon?

Hong Mei couldn't focus on any of the questions filling her head. Lao Ming had said her mother and father were both safe. At the moment, that's all she really wanted to think about. She drifted over to the wardrobe as if she was walking on air, and climbed inside to wait for Ryan and Alex.

After Lao Ming brought the brothers back to the room, Hong Mei listened from inside the wardrobe. She heard Lao Ming say in English, "Lao Ming sleep here, right outside door." There was silence from the boys. "Lao Ming keep you safe tonight," the old man said before Hong Mei heard the door close and the click of the lock.

She opened the closet door slowly and said, "Ryan? Alex?"

The boys yelped and jumped back.

"Do not be afraid. It is me, Hong Mei." The room was dim, but she could see the look of shock on the brothers' faces. She put a finger up to her mouth and whispered, "Shh."

Ryan ignored it and stomped toward her. "You've got something that doesn't belong to you. Give it back!"

"Please," Hong Mei said, panicking. "Madam Ching must not know I am here. Be quiet!" she whispered hoarsely.

Alex stood by the door with his arms folded across his chest.

Ryan rushed at Hong Mei and said, "I don't care —"

She didn't let him finish his sentence. Reacting to his

aggressive move toward her, she automatically responded with a basic "bridge-smashing technique." The *gong fu* move pushed Ryan's energy back on him, and sent him tumbling across the wooden floor.

Huh! She hadn't lost her skills.

Spread out on his back, Ryan lifted his head and stared at Hong Mei.

Alex gasped. "Hey, how'd you do that?"

Once again, Hong Mei raised her finger to her mouth. She looked quickly at the door and said in a loud whisper, "We are in great danger. Please, listen carefully."

Ryan sat up and shook his head. In a low voice this time, he said, "You've got a lot of nerve. First, you steal our jade, leaving us some old box. Then –"

Hong Mei interrupted him. "You saw the box? Did you read the poem inside?"

"Read the poem?" Ryan asked, standing up and brushing off his clothes. "As if we were in the mood for reading poetry after discovering our family heirlooms had been stolen!"

Hong Mei saw Alex moving over to the bureau.

"I will give you back your jade, but you must listen," Hong Mei said. "Lao Ming will try to protect us, but if Madam Ching –"

Ryan interrupted her again. "Yeah, right. That guy couldn't hurt a flea."

"Lao Ming is on our side. He is a friend of my father's."

"Oh, and who might your father be? They certainly hadn't heard of him at that hotel in Kowloon!"

"Ryan, please. I am sorry. Let me explain."

"Sorry?" Ryan looked incredulously at her. "Look. I

don't know who you are. All I know is that I want our jade back. And as soon as I get that, I'm going back to Hong Kong and straight to the Canadian Embassy. Madam Ching is a kidnapper and a murderer. If you don't get us out of here, I'll make sure you get arrested for being an accomplice."

"Please," Hong Mei said. "I beg you. Listen."

Alex had come up and stood next to her. He held the box with its lid broken off and said, "If I give this to you, will you give us our jade back? Madam Ching wrecked it, but I think you could glue it back together."

Hong Mei felt her heart trip at Alex's words. She immediately reached into her pockets to retrieve their jade and give them back. When she took them out, she saw the boys' eyes light up. Holding them in her hands again, she marvelled again at how beautiful they were. She remembered how gorgeous it had been when it was one whole piece. She didn't really have to give them back, did she? Perhaps she could keep them awhile longer.

The sound of Ryan clearing his throat brought her attention back to reality. Whew! She felt dizzy. Looking at Alex as he held the box in his hands, she remembered what he had just said. The poor kid was probably so scared, but here he was trying to be brave and help his brother get their jade.

Hong Mei shook herself. She needed to think about who she was and what she was really made of. She *knew* that she could be bigger than this.

"Do not worry about the box now," Hong Mei said gently. She held all three pieces of jade out toward the boys. They snatched their jade out of her hands, ignoring the third piece. Alex studied his and she watched Ryan lovingly trace the etchings on his. They laced them onto their cords and tucked them inside their shirts.

Hong Mei took the container that Alex gave her. It wasn't broken too badly. She felt her heartstrings pull again when she saw her poem.

A few moments later she said, "Lao Ming thinks this box is very special."

Ryan gave her a withering look. "Madam Ching didn't seem to think so."

Hong Mei felt her face turning scarlet.

"Yeah," Alex said. "When Ching Long brought us here from the train station, Madam Ching –"

"I do not understand," Hong Mei said. "When were you at the train station?"

"That's where we ended up," Alex said. "We got on the subway in Hong Kong, and the next thing we knew we were in Beijing, like, thirty minutes later."

Is this what Lao Ming meant? Had Master Chen's box brought them here? "Tell me what happened," she said.

"So, we were just sitting on the train," Alex said, "watching the different stations go by. Ryan couldn't decide which one we should get off at."

"Well, you were no help," Ryan said.

"And?" Hong Mei asked.

"We were, like, sitting there and I was holding the box. Just like this," Alex said taking the box from her to show her. He held the box in one hand and the lid in the other.

"That is it? You were not doing anything else?"

Alex said. "Well, we recited Papa's poem about then, I guess."

"Can you say this poem again?"

"I don't see —" Ryan interrupted.

"Please. If the box brought you here, perhaps it can take us back to Hong Kong."

"I thought you said Lao Ming was on our side," Alex snorted. "Why doesn't he just get us out of here?"

"Because Madam Ching will kill him."

Hong Mei felt Alex come closer to her. "Ryan? Please?" he asked in a squeaky voice.

Ryan took a breath and looked from Alex to Hong Mei and back to Alex again. He sighed, but started reciting the poem. Alex quickly joined in.

It sounded like the same one she'd grown up with, but their words were in English. When they came to the last lines, the floor began to tremble. A second later, the beds, dresser and wardrobe shook and shimmied across the floor.

"Was this what happened on the train?" Hong Mei asked, trying to keep her voice steady as she was trying to keep her balance.

"No," Alex stammered.

"Yeah, this feels like an earthquake," Ryan said. "Quick, get on the floor!"

Hong Mei didn't need to be told again. The last time an earthquake had hit the region was only two years ago. Dozens of people were killed and hundreds of homes destroyed. And that had been a small earthquake. They were usually far deadlier.

The three of them scuttled for cover under the two beds. As the room heaved up and down and side to side, Hong

Mei, Ryan and Alex covered their heads with their arms.

As quickly as it started, the upheaval came to a stop, but Hong Mei said, "We should stay where we are for a little while. There may be more."

Hong Mei heard Alex ask Ryan, "Is this what it'll be like if we have an earthquake in Vancouver?"

"I guess so."

"But why didn't the box work? How come we're still here?" Alex groaned.

"I don't know," Hong Mei said, "but Lao Ming will probably check to make sure we are fine."

They stayed under the beds waiting for the old man to unlock the door and come in.

They waited and waited, but Lao Ming didn't come. Nobody did.

Finally, Hong Mei decided to try call out to Lao Ming. Perhaps he'd been hurt.

She crawled over to the door and reached up to the handle. It wasn't locked anymore and turned easily. Hong Mei stood up, opened the door and peered into the darkness. She found it hard to see. "Lao Ming?" called quietly.

There was no answer.

Hong Mei tried again, this time more loudly. "Lao Ming? Are you here?"

There was only the echo of her voice.

Hong Mei stepped out of the door to where the court-yard should be, but the ground felt different. There were no cobblestones, only bare ground. Directly in front of her was a high, stone wall. She looked up, but instead of the night sky, there was a huge, open-beam ceiling overhead.

Way up, dangling from high above, was a row of dimly lit light bulbs.

Ryan had come to stand beside her. Alex joined them, the box held tightly in one hand.

A low, crunching rumble came from behind them. Turning, Hong Mei saw that a huge, flat boulder now stood where the doorway had been. They appeared to be in a very large hallway with no visible exit.

"I was wrong," Alex said. "It *did* work."

CHAPTER 18

The Imperial Tomb

THE AIR SMELLED DRY AND DUSTY in the dark, walled-in area. Ryan wasn't able to see over the barrier, but he could easily make out the rafters and industrial lights hanging high above them. The cavernous ceiling reminded him of the inside of an airplane hangar. Stretching his hand out to touch the wall in front of him, he was reminded of the climbing wall in the gym at his school. Ryan felt the roughness of the rock-like structure with his palm, then made a fist and knocked on it. This was different than the one at school. The wall here was thicker and made no sound when he hit it.

"What is this place?" Ryan heard Alex ask. The quiver in his brother's voice scared him.

"I don't know," Hong Mei said. "Was it the same on the subway? There was no ice? No freezing wind?"

Ryan and Alex shook their heads. The three of them looked at the box that Alex still held. He thrust it at Hong Mei, who took it after hesitating for a moment.

As Ryan stood wondering about the box and how it worked, he noticed that Hong Mei had shifted her attention to where they stood. He watched her squinting, first left, then right, into the strange, half-lit corridor.

"Which way do you think we should go?" she finally asked.

"It's like being in one of those corn mazes," Alex said. "You can't tell which path is right unless you try it."

"I hope this isn't like that," Ryan said. "The last time we were in one of those, it took us forever to find our way out."

Hong Mei pointed to their right and began walking. "Let's go this way."

The boys shrugged, then followed her, with Ryan trailing Alex.

After fifty metres or so, they finally came to an opening in the wall. They turned left into another section of hallway. Their footsteps were muffled, but the ceiling still loomed large overhead. Was it an indoor maze for people to explore?

After another few steps they came to a sharp turn. At the end of it was an open metal staircase leading up. Hong Mei and Alex ran up the few steps while Ryan followed slowly behind. He watched as the two of them reached the last step and moved away from the stairs. Was it another level?

When Ryan was almost to the top step, he could see that Alex and Hong Mei were standing on a platform. Both of them were leaning on a heavy metal railing, gawking at something they hadn't been able to see when they were below.

"What?" Ryan asked, gripping the railings on either side of him. He didn't know if he wanted to keep going up. "What is it?"

"It is just like in the school books," he heard Hong Mei say.

"What is?" Ryan asked, taking one more step.

"Ryan!" Alex turned to him, his face in a huge grin. He waved madly for his brother to come up the rest of the way. "It's amazing! There must be hundreds of them."

"Hundreds of what?"

"Stone soldiers," Hong Mei said, still staring.

Stone soldiers? What were they talking about?

"Come up!" Alex was bouncing as he spoke. "It's exactly like that program on the Discovery Channel!"

Ryan walked up and moved slowly over to the metal railing where Hong Mei and Alex stood. They were in a hangar, but this one wasn't for airplanes. This one had been specially built to protect an army: one that had guarded an Emperor for more than two thousand years. Down below stood row upon row of life-size clay warriors, chariots and horses. Ryan felt his fear switch to awe. "The Terra Cotta army," he gasped.

He, Alex and Hong Mei stood silently at the railing, taking in the spectacle of perfect lines of infantry, archers and officers. Some men were crouching while others were in standing poses, but everything, including animals and men, looked remarkably lifelike.

Finally Hong Mei said, "I see some stairs over there." She pointed to another set of metal steps leading down into the pit below. "Should we go and look more closely?"

"Okay," Ryan said at the same time as Alex.

"Follow me," she said, leading the way.

Taking the stairs down, they stopped in front of the first statue they came to.

Ryan looked almost eye-to-eye with the lifelike statue. The warrior's noble and steady gaze stared back at him. Ryan thought that the way the man's thin moustache curved above his unsmiling mouth made him look like he was hiding a secret. He wore no helmet, but his torso and arms had been intricately chiseled to display fine armour. He was poised to fight.

Ryan, Alex and Hong Mei moved forward, studying each sculpture that they passed. Just like real people, some were tall and slim while others were short and heavy. They wore different uniforms and hairstyles, and on some, Ryan could see remnants of the coloured lacquer that once would have covered them.

After passing by many statues, Alex said, "Each one looks like it's got a different face. Do you remember that program, Ryan? It said that a different man had to sit and model for each one for the sculptor."

"Yes," Hong Mei added. "And, these −" She stopped and asked, "What do you call this stone?"

Ryan said, "Terra cotta or clay."

"Yes," she continued, "these clay men were buried with real weapons, but they were stolen a long time ago."

"Is it true that some people were buried alive after they worked on this?" Ryan asked.

"Oh, yes. Many," Hong Mei said.

"Buried alive?" Alex whined. "You mean there're dead people here? We're in a cemetrey?"

Ryan couldn't believe how stupid he'd been. Why had

he said that? *He* felt weird. How must his little brother feel? Alex wasn't stupid. He knew this place wasn't a replica of a tomb. This was a *real* mausoleum. And they weren't in Beijing, Hong Kong or Kowloon. The three of them were in Xian, practically in the middle of China.

He saw Hong Mei look at Alex, who had started to shake. "Are you all right?" she asked him, moving closer.

"I'm scared," Alex said hugging his arms around himself, shivering. "I want to get out of here. I want to go home!" he said, turning his face away.

Ryan moved to his brother and put his arm around him. Could things get any worse? First they get — what could he call it — *sent* to Beijing. Then, they get *sent* here to Xian, where the famous Terra Cotta Warriors were discovered. Why? If that old box was transporting them to different places, why had it brought them to *these* places?

He watched Hong Mei walk over to a large canvas tarp that had been thrown into a corner. Probably left by some archeologists wanting to get out of here and start their New Year holidays.

Hong Mei beckoned to Alex and said, "Here, let me cover you with this."

Alex went over to her and she said, "Please, sit."

Ryan watched as Hong Mei kneeled down and patted the ground beside her. Alex sat down and she pulled the heavy, stiff cloth around his shoulders. Looking up at Ryan she said, "Please, sit down."

"Thanks, but I think I'll stand."

"Please," Hong Mei said again. "It is time to tell you everything. I wanted to do this in Kowloon, but I could not."

"Maybe that's because you ditched us there," said Ryan.

"Please. Let me explain," Hong Mei said.

Alex huddled under the tarp and looked up at Ryan.

What choice did he have?

Ryan plopped down next to Alex, who immediately offered him a share of the tarp.

"I hope this doesn't take too long," Ryan said. "I want to find a way back to Hong Kong and our family."

Hong Mei took a deep breath and began to talk. She told them about the interview, meeting Madam Ching and seeing an ancient scroll. She told them about her relative Master Chen and about having visions.

She looked down at the box in her hand and said, "Madam Ching told me that this box was to store the jade in, but she couldn't have known it had such power." Reaching into her pocket, Hong Mei took out her jade.

Ryan could see that it was the same shape as his and Alex's. He automatically reached up to make sure his own pendant was where it should be.

"Why did you steal our jade?" Alex asked.

Hong Mei held her jade out for Ryan to see.

He took it. It did look a lot like theirs. Same shape. Same colour. Same edging. Even the etching on it looked similar.

"I didn't mean to take it," Hong Mei said. "Its power was very strong and I couldn't resist."

A kleptomaniac, Ryan snorted. How about that? They were stuck in a tomb in the middle of China with a klepto. Who was ever going to believe this one? He tried to laugh, but couldn't.

Ryan reached for his own jade to compare his and Hong Mei's. The more he studied it, the more he could see that Hong Mei's jade really could be the missing piece their uncle had told them about. When he put them side by side, they looked like they would fit. Together they looked brighter and more green.

"So you took our jade and left us the box. Did you know that it would do this?" Alex looked around and shivered.

"I did not know the box was magical until Lao Ming told me. But he didn't have time to tell me exactly how it works. I do not know why the box takes us where it does. Do you?"

"No," Alex said slowly.

Ryan caught the hesitation in his brother's voice. "Alex? Is there something you're not telling us?"

"Well, no," Alex stammered. "It's just that there was a 'truth' box in one of Uncle Peter's stories."

"What stories?" Ryan demanded.

"You know. From the scroll that Papa used to have. The one that got destroyed in the fire – stories about Black Dragon and the legend of the jade, stuff like that. He wanted to tell you, too, but he thought you'd only get upset. You know. Mama and Papa, and all."

"What? What about Mama and Papa?"

Ryan felt his heart speeding up as he stared at Alex.

"No, Ryan. Not about *them*," Alex said softly. He sighed and looked down. "Don't get mad. I'm just telling you. That's why Uncle Peter didn't want to say too much. He knows how superstitious you are and how – angry – you were at me. He didn't want to make it worse."

Ryan's head was beginning to hurt. He reached into his pocket and took out the tin of peppermints he'd put into his trousers. After taking a mint he passed the box to Hong Mei and Alex. Both of them took one.

"So what do you know that I don't?" Ryan asked.

"That the jade has to be returned to Black Dragon by midnight of the Year of the Golden Dragon." Alex removed his jade pendant and handed it to Ryan. "Just look at those three pieces. Do they fit together?" Alex asked.

Staring down at the jade, Ryan saw that they *would* fit. And each was glowing softly in his hand.

"Please be careful not to put the jade completely together," Hong Mei said.

Ryan looked at her. Her face had coloured and despite being in the cold building, there were traces of sweat above her lips.

"Why not?" he snapped.

"Ryan!" Alex said. "You don't have to bite her head off."

"Just because you think you know something I don't —"

"I don't *know* anything," Alex said, sitting up. "But I *think* Hong Mei might be right. Maybe the tale is true. Papa said our jade belonged to an Emperor, so maybe there are other parts of the story that are real."

"We must not forget the most important part. The jade belonged to Black Dragon. And to Black Dragon it must be returned," Hong Mei said, her eyes still focused on the jade in his hands.

Ryan didn't like the way Hong Mei was staring, and the peppermint hadn't helped his pounding head. He held her jade out for her to take. She snatched it. Alex glumly took his back.

The three of them sat quietly for several moments until Hong Mei said, "We must try to understand why the box has led us here to Xian. There is nothing in the scroll about that. What did your uncle call it, Alex? A 'truth' box?"

"Yeah. He used to tell me a story about Black Dragon and an old man. I guess he was Master Chen, your relative. Well, Uncle Peter described him as kind of a wizard-type guy. He, like, made this special kind of box to keep Black Dragon's jade in."

Ryan heard the words "wizard-type guy." Could his brother really have said that? The kid who always told Ryan that *he* was too superstitious?

"Master Chen was the man I told you I had a vision about," Hong Mei said. "He was my great-great – many times – great-grandfather," Hong Mei said.

"Oh, okay. I'm actually starting to get this," Alex said. "Anyhow, Uncle Peter said that only one of the heirs, usually the younger one, like Uncle Peter or me, would learn about the 'truth' box. I guess it was to protect us, in a way. I guess that's why Madam Ching didn't know about what it could do."

"And you did?" Ryan snorted. "Since when?"

"Ryan, please stop! I didn't really believe any of it either. It just seemed like kind of a cool secret that Uncle Peter and I shared. It wasn't until we ended up in Beijing and I figured out who Madam Ching was that I started to really think about things."

Ryan's head really hurt now. Why would Madam Ching have done something like that? What kind of a person would set a fire that was sure to kill people?

He caught snippets of what Hong Mei and Alex were saying: First Emperor, Black Dragon, power of the jade, a promise, fulfilling their duty. It was all stuff from the poem. Ryan reached up to massage his aching head and felt the beginning of a scab where that man had burned him. That man. Ryan swallowed and focused on Hong Mei and Alex.

"Hong Mei?" Ryan asked. "Do *you* believe that Black Dragon really existed?"

She nodded and said very slowly and quietly, "I believe he still exists. I have seen him."

Ryan felt himself shudder. "I think I've seen him, too."

Alex grabbed Ryan's arm. "You have? Where?"

Ryan sighed, "Do you remember that weird guy at the airport that I told you about, the one with the scary eyes?"

Alex frowned. "Kind of."

"I think he and the man who chased us into the subway in Kowloon are the same person." Ryan could feel his brother staring at him, but his head hurt too much to turn it.

"Do you mean the one who was howling after we jumped onto the train?" Alex asked.

"I think so," Ryan said.

"What does he want with us?" Alex asked.

"It is not *you* that he wants," said Hong Mei. "He wants our jade. It belongs to him. Perhaps he wanted to frighten us, to make sure we would be afraid to fail. He wants us to feel what his anger would be like if we do not give him the jade as promised."

"But if the legend is true, he's going to die with or

without the jade," Ryan said. "Right?"

"Well, yes." Hong Mei said.

Ryan continued, his head pounding. "He'd be angry, or disappointed or whatever, but he'd still die." He massaged his forehead. "My jade is the only thing I have left of my father. I don't know about you two, but *I* don't really want to give my jade away; especially not to someone like that awful man."

Hong Mei looked as if she was considering this. Ryan watched her put the box into her pocket before starting to bite one of her fingernails.

"It was a great sacrifice," Hong Mei said dully. "He broke his jade and gave up his chance at immortality."

"So what?" Ryan said. "It has nothing to do with us. That was two thousand years ago."

Neither Alex nor Hong Mei said anything.

Ryan pushed his glasses up. Even the bridge of his nose ached.

"I am afraid that if we do not fulfill Master Chen's promise, our jade may only bring us trouble, perhaps more death," Hong Mei said quietly.

"What do you mean, *more* death?" Ryan asked.

Hong Mei and Alex stared at him in silence.

The realization hit him like a sudden slip on black ice. Madam Ching had killed his parents. She'd killed them for his and Alex's jade.

Ryan felt anger bubbling up inside of him. His parents had died for two flat green stones. Reaching up with unsteady hands, he undid the clasp holding his pendant. What had seemed so dear to him a few moments ago suddenly seemed to burn the skin on his chest.

"Alex, take off your jade and give it to Hong Mei," Ryan said. His headache had turned to thunder. "She can do whatever she wants with it." His voice caught in his throat. "I don't want anything more to do with *this,*" he said, letting the fan-shaped jade fall into Hong Mei's already outstretched hand. "Hurry up. Give it to her and let's get out of here."

"I can't," Alex said looking up at him.

"What do you mean, 'you can't'?" Ryan cried.

"That's not the way we're supposed to do it, Ryan. *All* three heirs are supposed to meet Black Dragon at the river in the capital. *All* three of us have to hand over the jade."

"Well, *I* am not going back to Beijing," Ryan said. "If you want to go and see that *witch* again, go ahead, but I'm heading to Hong Kong."

His younger brother's eyes blazed. They sat, with eyes locked on each other's faces, for almost an entire minute.

Finally Alex said, "Okay. But just remember that this was *your* idea," he said, removing his jade and handing it over to Hong Mei. "Whatever happens will be your fault."

Suddenly, there was the distant sound of a door slamming somewhere in the building.

He, Alex and Hong Mei looked at one another.

Hong Mei pointed to the tarp. "Quick. Cover yourselves with that."

Ryan was instantly alarmed. Was this another trick?

"What are you going to do?" he asked.

"I will go see who it is. Perhaps it is the night watchman."

"What if it's not?" Alex asked.

"Just stay under there. I will come back as soon as I find out what made the sound."

Ryan watched Hong Mei open her hand with his and Alex's jade. She reached into her pocket and took her own out and added it to the other two. "Keep the jade. That is how you will know I will return for you."

He didn't reach out to take them, but Alex did.

Ryan looked at Hong Mei. One part of him said that he couldn't trust her and another said he had no choice.

There was the sound of a door again but he couldn't tell if it came from the same place or not. "Okay, but don't take too long," he mumbled. "I meant what I said, Hong Mei. As soon as you come back, Alex and I are out of here."

To Alex, he said, "Don't get any ideas. We're only keeping the jade as collateral. It's drenched in blood."

CHAPTER 19

A Historical Question

FTER HONG MEI had covered Ryan and Alex with the tarp, she made her way toward the sound. It was the middle of the night and nobody should be in the mausoleum. She hoped it was just a guard and they could stay clear of him.

Slowly, and as quietly as she could, she moved amongst the Terra Cotta Warriors. The soldiers were amazingly real, and the other figures were equally lifelike. Hong Mei could make out the defined muscles on the horses that stood proudly beside their riders. She marvelled at the intricate details etched on each of the full-size chariots that she passed. Hong Mei could only imagine how majestic the army would have looked when it was first painted in its glorious colours.

Lost in wonder, she was startled when she heard something behind her. Wheeling around, Hong Mei saw that nobody was there. She listened carefully, but could only hear her heart pounding in her ears.

Alex was right about this place feeling spooky. The soldiers seemed to watch her every move.

After taking a few more steps, she stopped again. Was this the way the three of them had come in? Hong Mei wished she had grains of rice to drop along the way, so she could find her way back to Ryan and Alex. Some leader she was turning out to be.

Hong Mei was about to retrace her steps when something thick and heavy coiled quickly around her ankles. She couldn't make out what it was and tried to shake it off. Her efforts were useless. Hong Mei called out for help from an unseeing clay soldier, just before she was yanked down to the ground and everything went black – again.

"Ah. Young Chen is finally waking."

Hong Mei was too groggy to place the voice. Her head throbbed. She swallowed and her throat burned with the effort. Opening her eyes, she tried to focus, but everything was blurry. She stretched her hand toward the figure and asked, "Who are –" but recoiled when she felt the dry, scaly skin. Now Hong Mei remembered who owned the voice.

"Black Dragon sees that Miss Chen is not well."

Hong Mei imagined the smirk behind the words. "How did you find me?" she groaned.

"Miss Chen is clearly not as intelligent as Grandfather Master Chen."

Drawing herself up to sitting, Hong Mei leaned against a cool wall. She could see better now, and noticed they were outdoors. Avoiding Black Dragon's eyes, she tried to speak again. "Where are –"

"Silence!" the man hissed. "Miss Chen only speaks when Black Dragon allows it."

Hong Mei smelled Black Dragon's rancid breath. She tried to breathe in some of the early morning air. Keeping her eyes averted, something in Black Dragon's hands caught her attention. The box. That's what had attracted him. Why hadn't she left that with the boys too?

"Has Young Chen recovered from her fall?" Black Dragon asked. He giggled. The high-pitched sound reverberated between her ears. It felt as if someone was poking around the inside of her head with acupuncture needles.

"Black Dragon longed to see his precious jade. Black Dragon worried that young Chen and the Emperor's heirs might try to cheat Black Dragon."

Hong Mei licked her lips. She glanced around without moving her head. Where was she? At her back was a cement wall and underneath her stiff legs were cobblestones. She and Black Dragon sat on the ground, but Hong Mei saw several stone tables and stools set up around her. Across the courtyard was a rolled-down shutter. *A tea shop?*

"Is Miss Chen listening to Black Dragon?"

Hong Mei leaned back and away. "Yes." She saw Black Dragon's nostrils flare. His forehead above the sunglasses wrinkled into a frown.

Hong Mei tried again. "Yes, Mighty Black Dragon. I am listening."

"Ahhh." Black Dragon sighed, and a smile forced his thin lips into a curve. "The girl is not so stupid after all."

Black Dragon stood up, towering over Hong Mei. She thought he looked bigger than he had at the airport. His robe fit tight, and the collar was undone. She saw the rough, dark skin of his neck. Black Dragon came within centimetres of her. Hong Mei drew her knees up as she tried to hide her fear.

"Black Dragon could no longer wait to see his jade. The jade that Black Dragon loved so much."

Hong Mei heard Black Dragon gnashing his teeth. She bit her tongue to stop her own teeth from chattering.

"And what did Black Dragon find in the box Master Chen made? The jade of Black Dragon? No. A piece of the jade of Black Dragon? No. There was not even the scent of the lovely green stone; only the taint of sandalwood, left over, no doubt, by the perfume of that evil empress." Black Dragon peered down at Hong Mei. "Miss Chen is trembling."

"Black Dragon – I mean Honourable Black Dragon. May I speak?"

He smiled and said, "Young Chen may."

"Madam Ching gave me the box, but –"

Hong Mei barely had time to cover her face as a searing blast of vapour shot out at her from the man's open mouth. She scrunched her body into a ball facing the ground, her arms wrapped over her head. Why had Master Chen told her not to fear Black Dragon when each time she encountered him he was so horrible to her? Black Dragon leaned down and continued spewing hot, fetid fumes over her while he spoke.

"Ching? Another Ching woman in this modern age? How did a Ching get her filthy hands on Master Chen's box? And why was she so foolish to give you this box?" His dark face turned blacker. "Are you telling Black Dragon the truth, Miss Chen?"

Hong Mei breathed in dusty air from the ground where she was huddled. This wasn't how a daughter of an ancient and mystical clan should end up. She pictured Master Chen's kind face and those of her loving mother and father, gathering strength from their images.

Using every bit of courage she could muster, Hong Mei pulled herself up again to standing. She straightened her back, stared Black Dragon in the face, and in a very firm voice said, "On my grandfather's honour, I am telling the truth, Great Black Dragon. Madam Ching could not have known the power of the box. She gave it to me to take it to convince the Emperor's heirs of their heritage. She did not give me the scroll. She kept that."

"Scroll? Does Young Chen refer to the writing of Master Chen?"

"I believe so. It is the poem that my father taught me and the heir's father told to them."

"How does a Ching have this valuable document? It was to be kept safe by the Emperor's descendants. Are *none* of the heirs fulfilling their obligations?"

"Benevolent Black Dragon, please forgive us. We have encountered many obstacles, but at this very moment, the Emperor's heirs are safekeeping Almighty Black Dragon's jade. We were tricked by Madam Ching once, but it will not happen again. Wise Black Dragon is right. Madam Ching is evil."

Hong Mei bent her head down and said, "She killed the parents of the heirs when she tried to take your jade from their home. That is where she got the scroll."

Black Dragon roared. "The Ching woman possesses the same bad blood of her ancestor, the wicked Empress."

"Esteemed Black Dragon," Hong Mei said. "We escaped Madam Ching by using Master Chen's box. She wanted us to use your precious jade to lure Noble Black Dragon to her. She wishes to trap Venerable Black Dragon in Beijing so that she can prove to the world that dragons exist."

Hong Mei cringed as Black Dragon fumed, forcing fast clouds of steam from his nostrils.

"Black Dragon cannot be held against Black Dragon's will," he said. "Like the Empress, the Ching woman understands nothing of others, be they human or animal. The only thing the Empress cared about was herself. She, too, killed those who stood in the way of what she lusted after." Black Dragon spat onto a pretty flowering tree in a pot beside him. It crinkled as if burned by acid. "The Ching women are disgusting creatures."

"Virtuous Black Dragon? May I ask a question?"

Black Dragon nodded sagely.

"Did Master Chen's box bring the heirs and me to Xian so that I would have the opportunity to warn Revered Black Dragon about Madam Ching?"

Hong Mei watched Black Dragon sneer. "Black Dragon is not afraid of a Ching. In fact, she might make a tasty appetizer. Is she nice and fat?"

Hong Mei gulped. "Does Magnificent Black Dragon wish for us to return to Beijing now, or wait until it is safer?"

Hong Mei saw Black Dragon frown.

"Miss Chen is brave – but not as bright as a Chen should be. Why would young Chen and the heirs go back to Beijing?"

"Wasn't that the promise?" she stuttered. "That we should meet Considerate Black Dragon at the river — at Enduring Black Dragon's familial home in the capital city?"

She watched Black Dragon shake his head and a smile began to curl his black lips. But this time, Hong Mei saw that it was not an evil grin, but one that was human-like, as if he thought she'd said something funny.

"Master Chen made the box to keep Black Dragon's jade safe, but it also helps in the discovery of truth. The truth box takes humans to where they are meant to realize a truth they need to know. Part of this journey is for the heirs, and another is for you, Miss Chen. But if young Chen fails in lessons of history, it will not be easy."

Black Dragon snorted. "I hope that you will prove your worth as an heir, though female, Young Chen. I truly wish that you do not let Black Dragon, and countless others, down tonight."

He tossed Master Chen's box at her.

Hong Mei caught the case and watched Black Dragon saunter away.

When he was out of sight, Hong Mei slumped down beside the bush Black Dragon had spat on. She could see where he'd burned some of the leaves and flowers. How ironic, she thought, looking more closely at the plant. The shrub was *mei-hua,* also called *hong-mei,* the one she'd been named after. It never failed. Even in the coldest season it still bloomed.

Hong Mei looked up and saw a sign with black characters written on it. She had been right. This was a café for the visitors to the Emperor's tomb. She doubted it would be open today, the day of New Year's Eve, no matter how significant the place was to Chinese history. *Lessons of history*...of course! She shook her head at her own stupidity. When the prophecy was made, "the capital" meant Xian. Beijing wasn't the capital two thousand years ago.

Hong Mei needed to get back inside and tell Ryan and Alex they didn't have to go back to Beijing. A sudden thought struck her. Had Madam Ching made the same mistake? Hong Mei paused, thinking hard. The woman had clearly told Hong Mei to bring the heirs to Beijing. Now, here they all were in Xian – with Madam Ching hundreds of kilometres away.

Hong Mei looked at her watch: 15:18:36. She threw back her head and laughed to the sky. Madam Ching had no idea where they were, and they had plenty of time. It was 8:42 in the morning and she was starving. She still had to convince Ryan to complete what they were sent here to do, but surely she could do that over some breakfast. She'd heard somewhere that a way to a man's heart was through his stomach. Hong Mei blushed. Where had that come from?

She set off to find her way back to the Emperor's heirs.

CHAPTER 20

A Filial Farewell

RYAN? Are you awake?"

"Hmm?" Alex heard the muffled sound of his brother's voice.

It was dark and smelly under the tarp, but at least it was warm. He and Ryan had fallen asleep while waiting for Hong Mei to come back. Jet lag. Sometimes it wasn't such a bad thing.

Alex threw back the stiff cover from over his head and breathed in the dusty, chilly air. He looked up at the windows at the top of the hangar-like structure and saw that it was getting light outside. He shivered. It was cold in this place. No central heating in tombs, he thought with a half-laugh.

Shivering again, Alex wished he was wearing his own clothes. The blazer Madam Ching had made him wear to that dinner wasn't as warm as his Roots jacket. That one had a hood. He guessed he'd seen the last of it. He pulled the scratchy tarp up around his neck and listened to Ryan's snoring.

Where was Hong Mei? If it was morning already, she'd been gone a long time. Maybe she couldn't find her way back to them. Or maybe the sound they heard had been a security guard and she'd been arrested for breaking and entering. He didn't want to think what Ryan was going to say when he woke up.

He felt around beside him for Master Chen's box. Not feeling anything but the ground, he pulled back the tarp and searched for it. Where was it?

"What are you doing?" he heard Ryan mumble.

"Uh, nothing." How was he going to tell Ryan that Hong Mei hadn't come back *and* the box was gone? Had she been lying? Was she really on Madam Ching's side?

Ryan sat up and took his glasses out of his blazer pocket and put them on. Smoothing his hair he looked around. "Where's Hong Mei?"

Alex cleared his throat and said quietly, "She's not back yet."

Ryan sat up straighter and looked up at the same high windows Alex had. "It's morning and she's not back yet?"

Alex cringed. Ryan was going to lose it when he found out she'd taken the box. How were they going to get back to Hong Kong?

Just then, Alex heard, "Ryan? Alex? Are you there?"

It sounded like Hong Mei. "Here! We're over here!" he called, but not loudly.

A couple of seconds later, Hong Mei came around the corner and smiled. "I am so glad you are here. I got confused about how to get back to you. I had to use my second sight."

"Yeah, right," Ryan said. "You've been gone for hours! How confused were you?"

Alex saw Hong Mei's smile disappear, but she didn't turn red like she had before.

"I was with Black Dragon," she said, handing Master Chen's box to Alex.

"I'm sure," Ryan said.

Alex watched his brother roll his eyes.

"And I suppose Black Dragon asked you nicely for the jade and you told him we'd be happy to go back to Beijing and return it to him there. Right?"

Hong Mei stood unsmiling, but Ryan's words weren't having much of an impact on her as far as Alex could tell.

She turned to Alex and said, "Black Dragon told me the same thing your Uncle Peter told you about the truth box. It takes people to places where they learn an important truth."

"Oh, really," Ryan drawled. "Since you took the box, and I don't remember you telling us you were taking it, what *truth* did you discover with it?"

Alex studied Hong Mei's face. She was holding up pretty well.

Hong Mei shifted her gaze to Ryan. "I'm not sure, but I think it is that we do not have to return the jade to Black Dragon in Beijing tonight."

"That's amazing!" Ryan said sarcastically. "But *I* could have told you that, too. Because Alex and I aren't going anywhere except for Hong Kong." He stood up and straightened his clothes. "In fact," Ryan said, brushing the dust off his jacket and looking at Hong Mei, "we're headed there right now."

Alex swallowed. There was no way Hong Mei was going to convince Ryan of anything now. He watched his brother take the peppermint box out of his pocket, and almost immediately his face changed. He frowned, his eyebrows pursed in a look of puzzlement.

"What?" Alex asked.

"I don't know," Ryan said, undoing the buttons on his jacket and opening it up. "There's something in this pocket that I didn't notice before."

Alex watched Ryan feel the lining where the pocket was. "Is it an extra button or something?"

"No, it feels like a battery or something has been sewn into the inside of the jacket."

"A battery?"

"Yeah," Ryan said. "Like a double A battery."

Alex looked closer. He saw something blinking in the cloth that Ryan was fiddling with. Was that a light?

"Ryan. Something weird is in there. Take it off."

His brother quickly removed the jacket and threw it on top of the tarp. Looking at the blazer Alex wore, Ryan asked, "What about yours?"

Alex thrust Master Chen's box into Hong Mei's hands and checked his own pockets. He felt two pieces of jade in the left one and one in the right, and – what was that? He felt a heavy, cylindrical object. Quickly unbuttoning the jacket, he pulled it away from his body. He could just make out the same faint red light. He withdrew the jade pieces and passed them to Ryan, then tore off the jacket and threw it on top of Ryan's. Alex's breathing had quickened and he took a breath to try and steady it.

Ryan suddenly said, "Ssh. Did you hear that?"

Alex listened. He hadn't heard anything and was about

to say so, when there was the sound of a voice – a female voice – speaking Mandarin.

The three of them stood perfectly still and listened.

It couldn't be!

Alex looked back and forth between Ryan and Hong Mei.

"She is searching for us," Hong Mei whispered. "She knows we are here."

Now came the gruff voice of a man. Alex heard a laugh, followed by a chorus of grunts.

Hong Mei took off the lid of the box. Alex could see that her hands were shaking. She was already reciting the poem. He immediately started saying the poem in English. Speaking quickly and softly, Alex looked at Ryan, who had joined in. The three of them, whispering in English and Chinese, raced through the poem.

They were nearly at the end of the recitation when a man came around the same corner that Hong Mei had turned just a short while before. He stopped and his eyes lit up.

Alex had never seen a bigger person in his life. He was a giant with a shaved head the size of a watermelon.

The man shouted out in Mandarin, "They're here!"

Alex could hear Ryan and Hong Mei still reciting. He closed his eyes, shutting out the giant, and continued with the last few lines of the poem that he was getting to know so well.

A rumbling sound began and the ground shook as it had before at Madam Ching's. They were just saying the final words when Alex opened his eyes to see that a Terra Cotta Warrior had come loose from its foundation. It tipped dangerously close to the huge man. He raised his arms in alarm, trying to shield himself from the falling soldier.

Other sculptures started to wobble – horses, standing guards and chariots. Through the swaying army and across the heaving ground, Alex spotted Madam Ching. She glared back at him with icy-cold eyes and started toward them, striding purposefully through falling statues and debris.

Alex felt Hong Mei grab his arm and shout, "Quick! Come with me."

The last thing Alex saw was a large horse-drawn chariot rolling in front of Madam Ching, immediately blocking her way.

Hong Mei pulled him along to follow Ryan. They ran, dodging tumbling warriors, guards, infantrymen and generals.

Then, as quickly as the turmoil had started, the ground settled and everything stopped moving. Some of the army was in disarray and other parts seemed untouched. It had been just like an earthquake. Maybe that's what it was, since they obviously hadn't gone anywhere. They were still in the Terra Cotta Tomb.

But still, they kept moving.

Finally, Ryan said, "Here. There's an exit."

Alex and Hong Mei followed him through a door leading into a dark, tunnel-like walkway.

After taking only a few steps, Alex sensed that the air was different. It was thicker, somehow, and close. Not fresh at all. Ryan and Hong Mei had already disappeared from view.

"Ryan," Alex called into the claustrophobic passageway.

"This can't be the way out." He stopped to turn around. This place was making his skin crawl. "C'mon, you guys. This doesn't feel right."

He heard Ryan say from further ahead, "Keep going, Alex. It's okay! Come and see."

See what?

"I can't see anything!" he called out. "Where are you?" Alex shivered. He was chilly, even colder than before. He hugged himself as he made his way toward his brother's voice. This had better be good.

"Keep coming," he heard Hong Mei say.

Alex took another few steps and finally saw two dots of pale green light shining ahead. In their glow he could make out Ryan and Hong Mei. His brother was holding up two of the pieces of jade and Hong Mei held the third. The jade's colour changed from the pale green flush to a milky white. It illuminated the inkiness surrounding them. As he walked toward them, the light became as brilliant as a new star. He could see all around the room they now stood in.

Alex joined Ryan and Hong Mei who were gazing with open mouths at their surroundings. Nothing could be more different than the dusty archeological site they'd just left.

The room was small, slightly bigger than his bedroom, but far, far more beautiful. It resembled some of the Asian temples he'd seen in his aunt's coffee-table books. The walls were painted in rich hues of red, green, blue, yellow and gold.

When Alex looked up, he saw a dome-shaped ceiling with a sun, moon and stars made out of pearls and gems.

The ground was tiled and shaped into a model of forests, mountains, pastures and rivers – like a mosaic. And across the room was a set of jewel-encrusted thrones where two finely carved statues sat.

The life-size carvings were different than those of the army outside the chamber. These still wore their original colours, preserved perhaps by the lack of fresh air in the room. Instead of armour, the male figure wore a long, regal robe made of small rectangular-shaped tiles. Alex immediately thought of the chain-mail that knights wore in the Middle Ages, except this was made of jade and not metal. The statue of the beautiful woman also wore clothes of richness and royalty, but hers did not include jade, only gold and precious stones.

"They must be the Emperor and Empress," Ryan said.

Alex moved closer to the figures. "Look. There are two smaller statues behind them."

Holding the jade up high, Ryan went towards them. The other sculptures were young boys, nearly as tall as they were. Alex peered into the stone faces and thought how uncannily familiar they were.

He moved closer to Ryan and leaned against him. "Don't you think those boys look a little too much like us?" he asked his brother.

Hong Mei came up behind them. "Alex is right. They do look very much like the two of you."

Alex nudged his brother. "Ryan?"

Ryan didn't respond as he stared wide-eyed at the Emperor and Empress.

A masculine voice, soft and low, interrupted them. "Ryan and Alex. We have longed to see you again."

Alex nearly stepped on Hong Mei as he and Ryan stepped back.

"Please. Don't be afraid," the voice said. "Listen."

He and Ryan stood together, trembling. They heard:

> Long before the universe was born,
> Chaos rose from a celestial storm.
> Alone for eons in an endless night,
> The god awoke and created light.
>
> Seeing the beauty of what he'd done,
> Chaos then made the Moon and Sun.
> His next major task was to give birth
> To all the planets, including Earth.
>
> After sprinkling stars across the sky,
> He looked to his wife; her frown caught his eye.
> What's this? he asked, You don't like what you see?
> Is something not right? Please – tell me.

The voice was so familiar. It continued on for a few more lines, then said, "You have grown into such fine young men. I am sorry that your mother and I cannot be with you. But I am glad that Master Chen's box has brought you here so that I can tell you how very much we loved you."

Alex felt Ryan's sobs before he heard them.

"Ryan, you have had a difficult time. Perhaps now that you have forgiven your brother you can find forgiveness for yourself. There was nothing you could have done to save us."

Ryan's shoulders shook. "I miss you so much," he cried.

"We know, but you must try to be strong, Ryan. You have your brother who needs you. And I know that your uncle and aunt care for you as if you were their own."

"I know," Ryan sniffled. "I will try harder."

"Good. And Ryan? You must promise me something."

"Anything, Papa."

"You must fulfill your duty and return Black Dragon's jade. Do not let our death be for nothing, son."

The voice was getting softer.

"Be brave and true so that you and your descendants will live long and peaceful lives."

"Wait!" Ryan cried.

Alex saw his brother's face was shiny and wet. "Please don't leave us again," Ryan said, choking on his tears.

"Ryan, you must forgive us as well. We didn't wish to leave you. Goodbye. We will always love you."

Alex crouched down beside Ryan who had slumped to the ground. He put his arm around his big brother's shaking shoulders.

"I'm sorry that I always blamed you," Ryan sobbed. "Deep down, I knew better." His voice caught. "I just needed someone to blame."

Alex nodded and held onto him.

After a little while, Ryan's breathing steadied and he reached into his pocket.

"Looking for this?" Hong Mei asked gently, walking towards them with the peppermint box.

Alex saw Ryan try to smile. "Thanks," he said, taking it from her.

He opened it up and Alex saw there were only three

mints left. When Ryan offered Hong Mei and him one, they said no, but he insisted, so they each took one. Ryan set the empty container at his feet while he retied his shoelace.

Alex popped the white peppermint into his mouth. "Are you okay?" he asked Ryan.

"Yeah. Are you?"

"Yeah."

After a minute, Alex turned to Hong Mei and asked, "So now what?"

"I think we should stay in here until it's safe to go out," she sighed. "I wonder how Madam Ching got from Beijing to Xian so fast."

"We've been gone all night," Alex said. "Even if she only discovered we were missing early this morning she could have got on a plane and flown here. Do you remember what Ching Long said? About one of her ex-husbands being a bigwig at some airline company? It would have been easy for her to get here."

"I guess," Ryan said. "So then, I agree with Hong Mei. Let's just stay in here until one of us can go out and take a look around. This room seems to be safe enough for now."

Alex smiled. "Does that mean you want to return our jade to Black Dragon tonight?"

Ryan smiled back. "Absolutely."

CHAPTER 21

Out of the Pot and Into the Fire

Hong Mei looked at her watch. The lit-up digits said: 11:25:36

Eleven hours, twenty-five minutes and thirty-six seconds until midnight. It was past lunchtime and she hadn't eaten this morning or the night before. If she was starving after meeting Black Dragon, she was ravenous now. She groaned. How much longer would they have to wait in here? Would she and the boys never agree on when it was safe to leave the royal chamber?

And not only was she hungry, Hong Mei was *so* bored.

She, Ryan and Alex had talked a bit, telling one another about their lives and what they liked to do in their free time. Hong Mei had suggested that they divide the jade up and put each piece in a different part of the room so they could have some light. Separated, it did not shine as brightly, but it still gave a warm glow. At least they could see one another while they chatted. Hong Mei told them about helping Mama on her rounds visiting patients and how they'd moved so much.

Compared to hers, Hong Mei thought Ryan and Alex's lives very simple and wonderfully easy. The only thing they *had* to do was get good grades in school. Neither of them worked. Ryan said he hung out with a few friends. Sometimes they went snowboarding but Ryan said that most of the time they would just meet in a restaurant or coffee shop.

Alex spent most of his free time riding and taking care of his horse. He made it sound like it was a lot of work, but Hong Mei thought he sounded too excited about it for it to be a chore. She'd never even seen a real horse, except for those poor things hauling carts in some of the villages she'd lived in. They were probably more mule-like than horses anyway.

And all the travelling these two did with their aunt and uncle! She hadn't been out of China, and Ryan and Alex had already been to five continents! It seemed like they really *did* lead royal lives.

After they had talked about their families for awhile, she and the boys had fallen silent. She thought that they were all probably thinking the same thing: how much they wanted to get this thing over with so they could all go home.

Hong Mei's stomach rumbled again. She pressed on it with her hands, trying to make it stop.

"You're hungry, too, huh?" Alex asked.

"Yes."

"Me, too. Do you think we should take a chance and go out there?"

"Do you think Madam Ching thinks we've left and has gone out to look for us?" Ryan asked.

"Or do you think she's left a guard or two behind?" Hong Mei asked. "I remember hearing more than one man's voice."

"I don't know," Alex said. "But I'm starving."

"Why don't I go out and have a look around? You two can stay here, just in case," Ryan offered.

Hong Mei knew she was supposed to be the leader, but she didn't want to run into Madam Ching or one of her people. She remembered Lao Ming telling her that she was lucky to have escaped from the woman's thugs at the airport. Sighing, Hong Mei knew this was no way for a Chen to think. She was the chosen one. She had dragon's blood. Her father believed in her.

"I'll go," she said, surprising herself. "I can sneak out and if it is safe I will get us something to eat. I think Ryan is right. This is probably the safest place for us to wait until we go out to find the river."

"Do you want me to go with you?" Hong Mei heard Ryan ask.

His words made her feel warm inside. "No," she stammered. "I can go alone." She looked at him and said a quick, "Thank you."

Hong Mei stood up and moved toward the tunnel-like entrance. As she approached it, she saw a beam of light dancing inside the corridor. She stopped and turned quickly around to the boys, raising her finger to her lips, motioning them to be quiet. They looked questioningly at her. She silently pointed to the tunnel where the light, bouncing off the wall, grew larger and more intense.

She held her breath and silently pleaded, "*Please, please go away. Don't look here. We're not here.*"

Her heart sank as shuffling footsteps followed the yellow flashlight beam that now swept the room. It went from Ryan to Alex and then to Hong Mei.

Hong Mei smelled sandalwood.

"Well, well, well," Madam Ching said. "What have we here?"

Ryan, Alex and Hong Mei each made a dash and grabbed their jade. Then they moved together and formed a group.

Madam Ching shook her head and snorted delicately. "Isn't that sweet? You've become a real team." She called back through the tunnel, "Ching Long? I'm in here, darling. Tell the others I need a hand."

Realizing that she'd left Master Chen's box at the feet of the Emperor and Empress, Hong Mei looked quickly to see if it was still there.

Madam Ching followed Hong Mei's glance and said, "Did you drag that old thing here with you?" Then she narrowed her eyes and asked, "Why?"

Hong Mei ignored her question.

Ching Long entered and flashed a winning smile at Hong Mei, Ryan and Alex. "Hello," he said brightly. "Fancy meeting you here."

Hong Mei noticed Alex trying to edge over to Master Chen's box.

"Son?" Madam Ching said. "Go fetch that old wooden box for me before that little imp gets his hands on it."

Ching Long pulled Alex back and pushed him away. He picked up the box and turned it over. The lid fell off. He leaned over and picked it up, saying, "Pity it's broken. It'd look nice in the library, don't you think, Mother?"

Then he moved over to Ryan and came within centimetres of his face. "Why is it that every time I see you and your little brother, you have this box? Special, is it?"

Two men entered the room. Hong Mei saw that one was Melon Head and the other was as huge as the first. They looked like sumo wrestlers. Together they barred the exit, their beefy arms folded over their massive chests.

Madam Ching pointed with one very long red nail at each of their hands holding the jade. "Take the jade from them, won't you Ching Long?"

Ching Long stared at his mother. "Me? Why must I touch it? Isn't it dangerous?"

"Darling," Madam Ching said, "You're not afraid, are you?"

"Mother," Ching Long said. "You've always told me that's what these three," he said, waving at Hong Mei and the brothers, "were for."

Madam Ching sighed loudly and rolled her eyes. "Why must I be surrounded by imbeciles?" Madam Ching asked. "Never mind, then." She pointed to the men by the door and said, "Get one of them to collect the jade and put it into the box."

Hong Mei watched Ching Long's nostrils flare as he looked at his mother. "*I'll* do it!" Ching Long said and moved over to pluck the jade from their hands before dropping them quickly into Master Chen's box.

"That's better," Madam Chen said. "I can't tolerate weak men."

"Please, Madam Ching," Hong Mei said. "You cannot keep the jade. We must return it to Black Dragon at midnight."

Hong Mei watched the woman's top lip curl. "From the beginning, Miss Chen, you have thought you were someone special. And I must admit, when you brought the Emperor's heirs here instead of joining them in Beijing as I ordered you to, I almost believed it. I should have known you might figure out that Black Dragon's ancestral home was here in the old capital and not the newer one." Her beautiful face turned sour. "But how did you manage to get here so quickly?"

She shook her head and her face resumed its haughty expression. "No matter. *You* are not the one in charge here. *I* am." She turned toward her son. "Now then. We've got everything we need to celebrate the Year of the Golden Dragon tonight. Black Dragon will be desperate to join us in the festivities." She waved lightly, but didn't bother looking back. "Bye, children."

Hong Mei looked from the boys to the exit and back to the boys.

Ching Long said, "After the men seal this place up, you should try not to move around too much. You don't want to waste oxygen. And don't bother wasting your breath calling for help, either. The tomb security guard has been...detained, shall we say, and won't be coming to work anytime soon."

Showing off his white teeth, Ching Long said, "Goodbye, then. Thanks very much for being of assistance."

He left and one of the two large men followed him out. The other giant blocked the doorway and glared at the three of them. His puny black eyes were almost lost in the folds of his fat face.

Grunting and groaning sounds came from the other end of the tunnel.

"They're not really going to leave us in here, are they?" Alex cried into the quickening darkness.

Hong Mei said, "It will be okay. Let's remain calm. We'll find a way out."

But how? she thought. Without Master Chen's box or the jade, they would have to try and dig their way out.

After only a minute or so, the man from outside called for his partner to go out. The man winked at the three of them and backed out of the room. Hong Mei heard scuffling and something being slid across the mouth of the tunnel. It was very dark.

Those men might have been able to push a few of the statues in front of the opening, but she could see light through the cracks and gaps. It faded as the men and their flashlights got farther away. Air could definitely come through the spaces – maybe not a lot, but enough. If she and the boys worked slowly at moving the stones from the opening, they could be free in an hour or two. Long before their air ran out. Couldn't they? They still had plenty of time before midnight to find Madam Ching again. She'd no doubt be at the river waiting for Black Dragon.

Hong Mei made her way with outstretched arms to where the opening had been. She felt the broken pieces of clay and stonework, then pushed on the barricade with her shoulder. It didn't budge. She pushed harder. Nothing.

She heard Ryan call out, "How long do you think it'll take to dig our way out?"

"I am not sure," she called back. "I will try something that my father taught me."

Hong Mei stood still and focused on her body and its energy. She started with her feet, and moved up the muscles in her legs. "I am strong," she said to herself. She thought about the strength in her hips and midsection. Drawing deep breaths, she imagined the air as power handed down through the ages from Master Chen to her father and now to her. She filled her lungs and emptied them. There was might in her chest and arms. She could feel it filling up the muscles, tissue, veins and arteries. Yes, she was very strong. She, Chen Hong Mei, could do this. She would move whatever was blocking the door. She could do it.

Thinking only of her purpose, Hong Mei pushed with all the energy and might that she possessed.

The barricade did not budge.

She tried again.

There was not even a slight shift.

Slumping down to the ground, Hong Mei started gnawing at one of her fingernails.

CHAPTER 22

The Emperor's Army

HONG MEI?" Ryan called. "I'm coming to help you."

"I am here, Ryan," Hong Mei said.

He made his way toward her voice.

"I've tried pushing and it didn't do any good," she said.

Ryan reached up and felt around, his fingers looking for cracks and loose rock. He wished he had something sharp that he could use to chisel with. That's what they needed. A chisel and hammer like sculptors used.

"Ryan?" he heard Alex approaching. "Can I help?"

"Yes. Let's all try," Hong Mei said.

Together, the three of them put their hands flat against the stone. "*Yi, er, san!*" Hong Mei called out and they heaved against the barrier.

They stopped when they saw that they had made no headway. Alex asked in a small voice, "Will we really run out of air?"

"No," Ryan replied. "We'll figure something out."

"Ching Long was only trying to scare us," Hong Mei said gently. "We have come this far. We will find a way."

"Right," Ryan said. "What time is it anyway? I can't see my watch."

Hong Mei said, "Mine says: 8:17:21."

"What's that in real time?" Alex asked.

Ryan pictured a clock face and counted backward from midnight. Was it nearly quarter to four already? He tried to keep his voice steady, "I think it's sometime in the afternoon," he said, thinking that wouldn't alarm Alex as much as saying it was nearly four o'clock.

"*Exactly* what time, Ryan?" Alex asked.

"Three-forty-five," he said softly.

"Let us not think of the time," Hong Mei said. "Let us concentrate on a plan."

The three of them sat quietly. Ryan thought about what he could use to chisel away the stone. Perhaps his belt buckle would help. Or his peppermint tin. He reached into his pockets. Not there. Oh, right. He'd put it down when he was tying his shoe next to the statues of the Emperor and his family. His wife and two sons, just like Alex and him. Royal sons. Heirs to the throne. *Huh?* That meant that, in a way, the Emperor's army was their army, too.

"I've got it!" Ryan practically shouted. "I've got an idea."

"What?" Alex asked. Ryan could hear the hope in his brother's voice.

"Let's try asking the army to help us," he said confidently.

"The army?" Alex and Hong Mei asked in unison.

"Yeah. We're heirs to the throne, remember? They've got to listen to our command."

"They're made of clay," Alex said.

"I know that," Ryan said. "But stranger things have happened. Remember us being sent here by Master Chen's box? The train from Hong Kong? Hong Mei ending up at Madam Ching's? Papa talking to us just a while ago?"

"We had the box and the jade for all those things," Hong Mei said. "I do not believe the army can help us without them."

"Can't we just try?" Ryan asked.

They didn't answer him.

"Do you have any better ideas?" Ryan asked.

Hong Mei said. "He is right, Alex. Let us try."

"Okay. So what do we do?" Alex asked.

"I was thinking that since I'm the eldest, I would be the first in line, right?" Ryan asked.

"Yes, that is correct," Hong Mei said. "So you should be the one to tell the army to help us."

Was this really going to work? What should he say?

"Doesn't he have to say it in Chinese?" Alex asked.

Did he? Yeah, Ryan guessed so. He thought about which words to use. He knew how to say *help* and *Emperor*. "How do I say *army* and *heir* in Mandarin?" he asked Hong Mei.

She told him and he cleared his throat. "I, Ryan Wong, heir of your Emperor, command you to help us. Release us from the royal chamber."

The three of them sat expectantly.

"Try it again, but louder this time," Alex said.

Ryan said the words over again, but much louder.

217

There was still no sound of movement from the mouth of the tunnel.

"Perhaps you should both say the words," Hong Mei said.

"My Chinese isn't good enough," Alex said. "I can't speak it like Ryan can."

"You just have to say a few words," Ryan said. "I've heard your Mandarin. It sounds better than you think."

"Well," he said. "If you think I can."

"Yes," Ryan said, "I know you can. Let's say it a couple of times before we shout it out."

He and Alex repeated the sentence twice, and then, on the third time, raised their voices and called out, "We, Ryan and Alexander Wong, heirs of your Emperor, command you to help us. Release us!"

The earthen floor trembled and there was a sound of stone scraping on stone. Ryan felt new air waft into the room.

"It worked," Alex yelped, jumping up. "Let's go!"

"After you," Ryan said to Hong Mei.

"You did it," she said, moving to him.

Ryan heard the surprise in her voice. As she walked past him, he caught her hand in his. She squeezed his fingers and tugged his hand for him to follow her.

When the three of them stood outside the royal chamber, they looked at the huge pile of broken clay and stone.

Alex said the words that they were all probably thinking. "I don't know if we would've got out without the army's help."

None of them said anything.

Finally Hong Mei looked up at the few skylights in the hangar. "It's getting dark. We had better find our way out and go to the river. Madam Ching must be waiting there for Black Dragon."

By the time they got outside and stood on the steps at the entrance of the tomb, it was those few short minutes between nearly dark and dark.

The three of them shivered in the twilight. Which way was the river: north, south, east or west?

"We need to go north," Hong Mei said.

"How do you know?" Ryan asked. "Have you been here before?"

"Not to this part of Xian, but I've been to where the old palace stood. I know a little about *feng-shui* and how people, particularly an emperor, would have had his homes set up. We are now on Lishan Mountain. According to tradition, the Emperor was buried in the eye of a dragon-like shape. The river should be to the north of us."

"How far north?" Alex asked.

"That, I don't know," she said.

"Well, let's get going," Ryan said.

"Do you think if we see anything to eat along the way, we can pick something up?" Alex asked.

"Yes," Hong Mei said. "Do you like Chinese food?" she asked.

"Not really, but I'll eat anything right about now," Alex said.

CHAPTER 23

Beauty and the Beast

"DO YOU FEEL BETTER NOW?" Hong Mei laughed as Alex rubbed his stomach.

He nodded, but his mouth was too full to speak.

Hong Mei, Ryan and Alex were standing beside a street vendor selling steamed buns stuffed with barbequed pork.

"They're a bit different than the ones we get back home, but they're still good," Ryan said, reaching for another one in the plastic bag he held.

"Yes, the kind Mama and I eat are also not the same," Hong Mei said. "Ours have different spices, I think." She sighed, wishing she was with her mother right now. Everyone around them — those standing in line to get pork buns or other savoury and sweet snacks, families sitting together in the restaurants along the street, or others who were making their way toward the river — were all with the ones they loved. Tonight was New Year's Eve, and no Chinese would dream of not being with their family.

Brushing off her hands, Hong Mei said, "We can at least thank Madam Ching for not letting us starve. That was the last of the money she gave me before I went to Hong Kong to meet you."

"That seems like a lifetime ago," Ryan said.

She nodded. He and Alex were probably feeling just as lonely as she was. "Yeah, well, let's not forget that she left us to rot in the royal chamber. Who knows if anyone ever goes in there?" Alex said.

The three of them looked at one another.

Ryan broke the silence. "It was quite a hike here. How much time have we got?"

Hong Mei looked down at her watch: 3:11:23.

"A little more than three hours," she said.

"Where do you think the old hag is, anyway?" Alex asked.

"She's got to be here somewhere," Ryan said. "But if we still have that much time until midnight, we'd better not find her too soon. No telling what she'd try next."

"I think we should go right down to the river, and stay out of sight there."

Alex bit his lip and said, "But what'll we do if we see her?"

"Nothing," Ryan said. "We just have to make sure she doesn't see us."

"What if Black Dragon sees her and not us, and thinks we're not coming?" Alex asked, his voice getting higher with each word that he spoke. "What if she shows him the jade and says we've let him down?"

"That's when we'll make our move," said Ryan.

"But he'll see that we don't have the jade! He'll see that *she* does!" Alex squawked.

"That is why we must stay hidden. We want to make sure to surprise Madam Ching *and* show Black Dragon that we have come as promised. We will tell him, in front of Madam Ching, that she stole the jade and means to keep it," Hong Mei said.

"Don't start freaking out now," Ryan said to Alex. "We've been talking this through the whole way down."

Hong Mei looked at the two brothers. They were lucky to have each other. She'd never really thought about having a brother or sister, but right now, she wished she had one.

"It's easy to talk about it, Ryan. I'm just scared it's not going to work," Alex said, his voice no longer squeaky, but very, very low.

"It is a good plan," Hong Mei said.

"It's our only plan," Alex grumbled.

"C'mon. Let's get closer to the river," Ryan said.

The threesome looked over their shoulders and left the outdoor food stall. They mingled with the hundreds and hundreds of other people making their way to the river. Everyone wanted to find a good spot for their families to watch the fireworks, set to start at exactly midnight.

Hong Mei looked at the other revellers and saw that everyone was dressed up in their new clothes. She thought about the red turtleneck and trousers that she'd been wearing for the last three days. They'd seemed so special when she and Mama had bought them.

Ryan must have seen the look on her face, for he came close and took her hand. "Are you okay?"

Her heart scrunched in her chest. "Yes. Are you?"

He sighed. "I'm just thinking about Uncle Peter and Aunt Grace. They've probably got every policeman in Hong Kong and Kowloon looking for us."

Hong Mei couldn't trust her voice, so she only nodded in reply. It must be terrible for the boys' family. At least her father knew what she might be up to, and had hopefully convinced her mother that she was okay. Maybe he could even see her with his second sight and would know that she and the other heirs were doing their best to complete their unenviable task.

Hong Mei looked at Alex walking beside her with his head down. Taking his hand, she squeezed it and smiled. He didn't return the smile or the squeeze.

After walking for about half an hour, they came to a walkway that ran along the riverbank.

Alex asked, "Why are there so many people down here?"

"They're waiting for the fireworks," Hong Mei said.

"Let's go over to that stone bridge and see if we can see Madam Ching," Ryan said.

"No, it is too open there. We still have," she checked her watch, "more than two hours. We must find her, but she cannot see us."

The three of them stayed close together and peered across the river and along the banks where they stood. They tried to stay hidden behind other people. Hong Mei was glad that more and more people were arriving.

Suddenly, Alex shouted, "Ryan! Look over there! Across the river!"

"What?"

"Have you found her?" Hong Mei asked.

"Not Madam Ching," Alex said, jumping up and down and waving, "Aunt Grace!" he shouted. "Aunt Grace!"

"What? Where?" Ryan stood up on tiptoes, straining his eyes to look for her.

"There, across the river. Do you see her hair? Over there. Uncle Peter is standing right beside her."

Hong Mei felt Alex pulling her hand.

"C'mon. Let's go," he started shouting out again. "Aunt Grace! Unc —"

Hong Mei clamped her hand over his mouth. "Shh! It could be a trap!"

Alex flashed her a hateful look as he pulled her hand away. "How can it be a trap? Madam Ching thinks we're still inside the royal chamber," he said.

Hong Mei pulled Ryan and Alex away from a few in the crowd who had begun to watch and listen to them. Most were probably curious as to why three Chinese kids were using English together. Hong Mei dragged them further away. The last thing she wanted was for them to draw attention to themselves.

"We don't know if Madam Ching knows if we have escaped or not," she said. "She might have discovered it and sent for your aunt and uncle."

"How could they get here so quickly?"

"I don't know," she said. Hong Mei looked at Alex's twisted face. He looked like he was suffering excruciating pain.

"Where are they?" she asked. "Can you quietly point them out to me?"

Ryan pointed through a space between several people in front of him. "Over there. Do you see that blonde woman? You can't miss her. She's the only foreigner there."

Hong Mei peered to the other side and easily spotted the worried-looking aunt and uncle. But her glance did not rest on them. She felt her heart fly up into her throat. Standing next to Aunt Grace and Uncle Peter was Mama. And Baba.

"My parents," she barely whispered. "My parents are also here."

She watched as the foursome across the water pointed and talked together. How did they all know to come here? Had Madam Ching tricked them?

"Please," Alex begged, "please, I have to go over there. They're here looking for us."

Hong Mei turned to see Alex grab his brother's arm. "Ryan, come on. They're right there."

Ryan's shoulders fell and his face crumpled. "I know, Alex. I see them, too." His voice cracked. "But we can't. We have to go through with this. Maybe Madam Ching brought them here and it's part of her plan."

Hong Mei stared across at her parents, longing to swim right over to them. She wanted to feel them next to her, saying that this was all a bad dream. She wanted them to say that she and Ryan and Alex didn't have to do any more. They could all just go home and forget this whole thing had ever happened.

She blinked hard, focusing on Baba's face. He'd aged, but still looked like the father she remembered. He turned toward her, as if he sensed that she was there. Saying nothing to the other three he was with, Baba looked straight into her eyes. She felt as if he had wrapped her in his arms and hugged her close.

She imagined his voice in her head, and his words were, "We are here for you. I believe in you."

Hong Mei felt her heart soar.

She looked at Ryan and Alex and said, "I think Lao Ming brought them here. It's not a trap. Our parents are waiting for us."

"How do you know?" Alex asked.

"I don't know how I know. I just do."

She saw Ryan and Alex frown at her.

Alex asked, "Are they going to help us?"

"No, they cannot," she said.

Hong Mei saw his face fall. Ryan must have too, for he put his arm around his brother's shoulder.

More and more people were crowding the riverbank now. Hong Mei looked at her watch: 1:22:39. There was a little more than an hour until midnight. Where would Black Dragon be?

She said out loud, "If you were Black Dragon, where would you wait for your precious treasure to be returned?"

Hong Mei saw Ryan thinking, but Alex kept looking longingly across at his aunt and uncle.

Ryan said, "We know that Black Dragon gave the jade to the Emperor while they stood on the riverbank. But that could be anywhere along here."

"Legends say that dragons live in the deepest part of the river. We've got to find that section, I guess," Hong Mei said.

"How are we going to do that?" Ryan said.

"That's easy," Alex said. He nodded over at the other side of the river, down a hundred or so metres from where Hong Mei's parents and their aunt and uncle stood. "Old Madam Ching's already got it figured out."

Hong Mei and Ryan looked across the river toward where Alex had nodded. There stood Madam Ching and Ching Long. Their helpers were nowhere to be seen. Had they also been "detained," like the security guard?

Hong Mei shuddered, but said in as calm a voice as she could, "Let us make our way closer to them."

Ryan and Alex both sighed, but they nodded in agreement. All three of them took another look at their families before Hong Mei led the way toward the bridge down-river. What would they do when they got really close to Madam Ching? Should they announce themselves and tell her they were there to help her?

No. She'd never believe that.

The goons weren't there. They could try to steal the box and run.

No, that was too risky. They couldn't possibly get close enough.

She nibbled at a fingernail. Master Chen had said Madam Ching was treacherous and evil. Hong Mei didn't know if she could be evil, but she could try to be deceitful. Hadn't Madam Ching got her way by lying to everyone?

An idea began to form in Hong Mei's mind.

They reached the bridge and raced across it, trying not to be seen by the two Chings. When they got to the other side, the three of them walked in single file and stayed close to the trees lining the path. Hong Mei could see Madam Ching and Ching Long. They did not look her way, but seemed to be concentrating only on the water in front of them.

She checked her watch: 42:39 – there were less than forty-five minutes left until midnight. Hong Mei peered into the dark water and along the riverbank. Would Black Dragon appear on land as he had before, or as the water-dwelling creature of the old tales?

They were close now, very close. Hong Mei could see that Madam Ching's usual poise had disappeared. She stood with her neck craned forward and her face furrowed with anxiety. Her hands were in constant motion as she wrung them over and over.

Ching Long paced back and forth between Madam Ching and the river, his eyes focused on the slow-moving water.

Alex came up beside her. "There she is," he said, staring at Madam Ching.

"Yes, I know," Hong Mei said. "It will be okay, Alex. I have a plan."

"You do? I hope it's a good one."

"Me, too," she said frowning.

"And which plan might that be?" growled a deep voice from behind them.

The three of them wheeled around to stare at Black Dragon. Alex grabbed Hong Mei's hand and squeezed so hard that she thought her bones would break.

Black Dragon still wore his sunglasses and his tight, old-fashioned tunic. But his skin had changed. He actually looked much more reptilian this time and only partly human.

"Mighty Black Dragon," Hong Mei said quickly. "May I introduce Ryan and Alexander Wong? They are the Emperor's heirs."

"Delighted," nodded Black Dragon. "Let us move away from the crowd, shall we?"

Alex pulled back and Ryan shook his head. She glared at them and whispered. "There is nothing to be afraid of. This is what we are here for."

"Now, now," Black Dragon said in his low, gravelly voice. "Whispering is rude. Come along, now."

Hong Mei pulled the reluctant boys along the path to a small break in the trees where Black Dragon led them.

After only a few steps, he stopped and turned to look at them.

"So, the heirs have come to honour their ancient ancestors by keeping Master Chen's promise."

Hong Mei cleared her throat, but hesitated. She felt Black Dragon move closer to her. "Miss Chen? Do you have something you wish to say?"

"Yes, Almighty Black Dragon." Ryan and Alex leaned against either side of her.

"What is it?"

"The Ching woman is here, Honourable Black Dragon. She is here at the river with your precious jade." Hong Mei saw Black Dragon pulling himself up taller. His tunic looked as if it was going to split open. "She stole Virtuous Black Dragon's jade from us and left us to die in the Emperor's tomb." Hong Mei rushed on, "We heirs escaped once more and have come here to fulfill our duty."

"And how will the heirs accomplish this, Young Chen?" he said. "You have only minutes left and you do not have Black Dragon's treasure."

Hong Mei felt the heat from his sentences and smelled the stench of his rancid breath.

"We will fight fire with fire," she said.

Black Dragon did not reply. He only looked from one heir to the other.

"The heirs have come far since Black Dragon first met them three days ago. I believe you will complete this task. Go well," he said. "Finish it."

Black Dragon moved away from them and slunk further into the trees.

Hong Mei and the boys all shuddered at the same time.

"Please tell me your plan is an excellent one," Ryan said to Hong Mei.

"It is. We go to Madam Ching," she said.

"Are you crazy?" Alex cried.

"No." she said. "But you've got to trust me." She looked from Ryan to Alex. "Do you trust me?"

Ryan looked back at her and stared unblinking into her eyes. Hong Mei had never felt someone look at her this intensely, but somehow it felt good. She returned his steady gaze.

"I trust you," Ryan said.

"I guess I do, too." Alex said. "I don't really have a choice, do I?"

"Let us go," she said, feeling her heart swell.

The three of them walked toward Madam Ching. As they approached her, she seemed to sense them coming and turned to them. The worried look that Hong Mei had seen on the woman's face instantly changed to one of fury.

Practically pouncing on them, she came within steps of Hong Mei, Ryan and Alex. "*What* are you doing here?"

"I am afraid that you underestimated us," Hong Mei said.

"Perhaps, but it doesn't matter now anyway. We still have the jade and as soon as Black Dragon makes his appearance −"

"Black Dragon has not yet come to you?" Hong Mei cried. "Why, we have already seen him."

"You have seen him? How can that be? We are at the very spot he once met the Emperor and he has not surfaced."

"Perhaps it is because you are not the ones who are supposed to be here. *We* were the ones to give back the jade."

Madam Ching's eyes flashed. "How dare you speak to me like that!"

"You are right," Hong Mei said. "It was not polite of me. We will be leaving now." She looked at her watch. "The fireworks begin at exactly twelve o'clock, right? That's less than five minutes from now." She smiled and turned to walk away, "Come, Ryan and Alex. Let's find a good place to watch the show."

"Wait!" Madam Ching said. "You cannot go!"

"Why not?" Ryan asked. "It's finished now."

"But what about the jade?" Madam Ching cried.

"It's too late. We didn't have it when we saw Black Dragon. He seemed sad, but he said it wouldn't have any power now anyway."

"You're lying!" Madam Ching screamed.

Alex shrugged. "Let's go, you two. We don't want to be with *her* when the fireworks start."

Madam Ching turned to Ching Long and yelled, "Do something, you idiot!"

Ching Long stood helplessly holding Master Chen's box. Madam Ching grabbed it and opened it up.

"Oh, look," Hong Mei said, peeking at the box from where she stood. "It's not even shining anymore. It must be dead already."

"No, it cannot be!" Madam Ching said.

The crowd had started counting down.

"You could keep it in your library," Hong Mei said, mimicking Ching Long's words.

Madam Ching threw the box down, sending the three pieces of jade flying out.

"Thirty, twenty-nine, twenty-eight –" the crowd roared.

"Shame," Hong Mei said, trying to keep as calm as she could. She could hear the beating of her heart over the sound of the counting.

"Fine," Madam Ching hissed. "Take it and call him back. There is still time to bargain."

As casually as she could, Hong Mei bent down and collected the three sections of jade, then gave Ryan and Alex theirs.

"Sixteen, fifteen, fourteen!" The noise from the people was tremendous. Everyone was watching the sky, waiting for the first blasts and bangs.

The three heirs held the jade up and Hong Mei called out, "Come, Black Dragon! We have your jade."

"Ten, nine, eight," Hong Mei, Ryan and Alex counted with everyone else.

Ching Long was standing away from his mother, his gaze shifting between the river and his mother's face.

"Seven, six – there he is!" shouted Alex, as a scaly, black head surfaced. The massive round eyes caught sight of Hong Mei and the two boys.

Madam Ching leapt forward and tried to snatch the jade from Alex. In a split second, she lay splayed on the ground. Hong Mei had always wanted to use that particular *gong-fu* kick – but there was no time to savour its effectiveness.

"Three, two, ONE. Throw it in!" she yelled, and Hong Mei and the Emperor's two heirs sent their jade flying up and into the water.

There was a crack and burst of brilliant red light. As thousands of onlookers watched the dazzling array of colours filling the blackness above, Hong Mei and the boys watched something even more fantastic. The three pieces snapped together and formed, not a flat disc, but a perfect ball of brilliant green jade.

Just as Black Dragon was about to snap it up in his jaws, Madam Ching flung herself at the jade in an effort to catch it before it hit the water. She missed and fell with a splash into the freezing river.

Black Dragon snapped up his precious treasure and sank beneath the surface. Madam Ching flailed in the river for one or two seconds. Then, Black Dragon's head reappeared and pulled Madam Ching down with him.

Hong Mei looked around. Ching Long had disappeared: only the old people from her interview in Beijing were still there, and they seemed to be the only ones in the whole, vast crowd to have seen something other than the fireworks. They stood staring, wide-eyed and open-mouthed, at the roiling river water.

"We're free!" cried Alex. "Let's go find Aunt Grace and Uncle Peter."

Ryan and Hong Mei clasped hands and grinned.

They started moving through the crowd and along the path towards where they'd seen their families.

"Hey!" Ryan said. "Check this out."

On the ground near where they'd spoken to Black Dragon lay a pile of clothes: a long, old-fashioned tunic, sunglasses – and a long black braid.

CHAPTER 24

The Year of the Golden Dragon

I SEE THEM!" shouted Alex, running ahead of Ryan and Hong Mei. She watched to see Alex leap up to hug both his uncle and aunt at the same time. Hong Mei could see that the woman was crying.

She spotted her own mother and father, and when she felt Ryan pull her, she broke into a run. In seconds, her mother's arms were around her. The slight medicinal scent that clung to her smelled gorgeous to Hong Mei. She opened her eyes to see Ryan being hugged by his aunt and uncle, the four Wongs standing in a tight embrace.

Mama let go of her and said, "We're so proud of you, Hong Mei. I'm so sorry I didn't trust your father enough to even try to believe him." She smiled at her daughter, then at her husband. "He says he has forgiven me, but what do you think?"

Hong Mei looked up at her father who beamed down at her. "As I told your mother, everything happens for a reason. This was the way it was meant to be."

Hong Mei fell into her father's waiting arms.

"I'm so sorry, Baba." Her voice was wobbly. "I'm sorry for keeping your jade. I'm sorry for not helping you. I'm sorry for not believing in you. I'm sorry for everything," she cried.

Her father held Hong Mei close to him and whispered into her spiky hair, "Dear daughter. Please do not say those words again. All is well now. Today, I am the proudest father in all of China."

"Are you no longer sad that I am a girl?" she asked.

He laughed. "I was never sad to have a daughter. I was only trying to make you strong. And, in light of what you've had to face, I think you were up to the task."

Hong Mei's heart felt as if it was going to explode. No moment in her life would ever be as great as this one.

"Now," Hong Mei's father said. "Let us go with the Wong family and welcome the Year of the Golden Dragon. It has started off rather well."

EPILOGUE

Fudan University, Department of Archeology
22/02/00

During one of the routine checks of the royal chamber, a foreign object was discovered. There were no Chinese characters on the tin box, only English.

Upon inspection, the container was found to be empty except for traces of a white powder. The substance is currently being tested, but it is believed to be the remains of peppermint candies.

Since this was found in an area that is not open to the public and is supposedly sealed off to everyone but myself, it is clearly a case of site contamination. This, together with the failure of our night watchman to show up for work on New Year's Eve, should raise the alarm.

Recommendations regarding stricter procedures on access and protocol will follow in due course.

Signed,
Dr. Zhu Gong-wei

Acknowledgements

For me, writing a novel was as if I had embarked on a journey that I hadn't appropriately prepared for. Most certainly I had a suitcase, but as I made my way from ideas, to drafts, then edits, submissions and SASE's, I realized I had packed only the bare essentials. Luckily, I met people along the way, who gave me or told me where I could pick up some of the things I didn't even know existed. Still, at some stages, it was a bit of an endurance test, just as it is when you travel to places without roads or railways. Sometimes, one needs to switch to other modes of travel (say hopping on a passing oxcart) or walking from the last bus stop along a dirt road, with only the light of the moon as your guide, to a few thatch-roof huts on a beach. You've heard it's there – you just aren't sure how and when you might reach it.

Many, many people have been involved in the creation of this book. 'Golden Dragon' would never have come to fruition without their help. From the beginning, my husband Stan was an unwavering supporter. Whether he actually believed I had it in me, we will never know for sure, but he made me think I did. As for my sons, Sebastian and Christian, who only read snippets while waiting for the 'real' book to come out – here it is. I set off to write a Chinese adventure story and it is finally done. Thank you to my best friend and sister, Niki, whom I coerced into reading drafts by paying for her massage therapy afterwards. And to her husband, Allan, and my nieces Georgia and Reagan, who open their home to our family every year so that we might enjoy Canadian summers together.

To my friends and fellow writers, Karen Shur-Narula and Marcia Kelly-Gerritz – thank you for the writing retreats in the mountains and sois of Thailand and the good-humored and heartwarming conversations about writing, families and life in general. Even when my stories fail to find an audience, I know that you two will continue to read my work and say, "Now that is the best thing you have ever written."

My gratitude goes to my late grandmother, Eva Sauder, who instilled and supported my love of books and reading from an early age. I continue to enjoy her rhymes and verse, as well as her father's, my great grandfather. In addition to these gifts, they passed along their memories of a young Canada. I gratefully acknowledge my parents who once asked me as I played in the sandbox at our house on 94th Street, if I was digging to China. I remember that day in the summer of 1965 as life-changing. Yes, I was not even four, but that in itself should be a lesson as to the power of words for children.

Xie xie Lydia for giving Chen Hong Mei her name. I haven't forgotten the writers of the North Shore Writers' Association and the many wonderful words they produced and I enjoyed reading. Thank you to Sonnet, who edited the first completed draft. A huge thanks goes to my editor, Laura Peetoom, who was wonderful to work with, as she really got it and made me work at my own revisions. And last, but certainly not least, Nik Burton at Coteau Books who gave me a chance. I'll always be grateful. Thank you all.

DATE DUE
